something like normal

Trish Doller

BLOOMSBURY

NEW YORK LONDON NEW DELHI SYDNEY

First published in the United States of America in June 2012
by Bloomsbury Books for Young Readers
www.bloomsburyteens.com

For information about permission to reproduce selections from this book, write to
Permissions, Bloomsbury BFYR, 175 Fifth Avenue, New York, New York 10010

Library of Congress Cataloging-in-Publication Data
Doller, Trish.
Something like normal / by Trish Doller. — 1st U.S. ed.
p.   cm.
Summary: When Travis returns home from Afghanistan, his parents are splitting up,
his brother has stolen his girlfriend and car, and he has nightmares of his best friend getting
killed but when he runs into Harper, a girl who has despised him since middle school,
life actually starts looking up.
ISBN 978-1-59990-844-1 (hardback)
[1. Veterans—Fiction.   2. Post-traumatic stress disorder—Fiction.   3. Family problems—Fiction.
4. Brothers—Fiction.   5. Love—Fiction.   6. United States Marine Corps—Fiction.   7. Afghan
War, 2001-—Fiction.   8. Afghanistan—Fiction.]   I. Title.
PZ7.D7055Som 2012   [Fic]—dc23   2011035511

Book design by Regina Roff
Typeset by Westchester Book Composition
Printed in the U.S.A. by Quad/Graphics, Fairfield, Pennsylvania
2   4   6   8   10   9   7   5   3

All papers used by Bloomsbury Publishing, Inc., are natural, recyclable products
made from wood grown in well-managed forests. The manufacturing processes
conform to the environmental regulations of the country of origin.

For LCpl David Backhaus
(and Andy)

Chapter 1

At the end of the concourse I can see a few kids from the high school marching band playing the "Marines' Hymn" and a couple old guys—their blues straining at the waist—acting as an unofficial color guard. *Jesus Christ, please tell me my mom didn't hire a band.*

Mom's arms are stretched wide, holding a sign painted in cheerleader-bright colors that says *WELCOME HOME, TRAVIS!* Tied around her wrist are the strings to a metric shit-ton of helium balloons. It's bad enough I have to come back to Fort Myers. This is worse. I can't pretend this whacked-out welcome wagon is for anyone else—I was the only Marine on the flight.

The sign crackles, crushed between us as my mom flings her arms up around my neck, standing on tiptoe to reach.

Balloons drift down and bump softly against the top of my head. There is a year and a half's worth of hugging in this one embrace, and I get the feeling that if it were an option, she'd never let me go again.

"Thank God you're home," she whispers against my chest, her voice breaking with tears. "Thank God you're alive."

I feel like shit. Partly because I don't know what to say, but mostly because I'm alive. "It's good—" The lie sticks in my throat and I have to start again. "It's good to be here."

She hugs me too long and strangers walking past touch my back and arms as they say *thank you* and *welcome home*, and it pushes me beyond uncomfortable. Common sense tells me these people in their Ohio State T-shirts and New York Yankees ball caps are just tourists. Regular people. But I've spent the past seven months living in a country where the enemy blends in with the local population, so you're never sure who you can trust. My position is vulnerable and I hate that I don't have a rifle.

"I need to get my bag," I say, and I'm relieved when my mom lets go. She thanks the color guard, hugs a couple of the band girls, and then we head for the escalator to the baggage claim.

"How was the flight? Did they give you anything to eat? Are you hungry? Because we could stop somewhere for lunch if you're hungry." She talks fast and too much, trying to fill up the silence between us. A metallic female voice tells us the local time and weather so tourists can reset themselves. My watch is still set to Afghanistan time, even though I've been in the States for a couple of weeks. I forgot, I guess.

"Clancy's was always your favorite," Mom says. "You used to love their shepherd's pie, remember?"

Anger ignites in my chest and I want to snap at her. Clancy's is still my favorite restaurant and I haven't forgotten I love shepherd's pie. Except her intentions are good and I don't want to be disrespectful, so I offer her a half smile. "I remember, but I'm not especially hungry," I say. "I'm tired."

"Dad wanted to be here to meet you today, but he had an important meeting," Mom continues, in a tone that makes me wonder if she believes what she's saying. Maybe she's talking about someone else's dad. "And Ryan has been working at the Volkswagen dealership until he leaves for college."

After his professional football career ended, my dad bought three car dealerships. When I was in high school, I'd have worked at the VW dealership for free, just to have access to the shop and the parts for my car. But since I was his disappointment son, he refused and I ended up working on a landscaping crew for eight bucks an hour. Figures Dad would give Ryan a real job.

"And Paige . . ." Mom's lips pinch into a disapproving frown as she trails off. My mother has never liked my girlfriend—correction, my ex-girlfriend. My mom thinks she looks cheap. I think Paige belongs on the cover of *Maxim* in nothing but her underwear, which is exactly why I was attracted to her in the first place.

Stowed in the bottom of my seabag is the one and only letter she ever sent me. It came in a care package with cigarettes, dip, coffee, and porn. Only Paige would soften the blow of a Dear John letter by sending it with the stuff deployed Marines want most.

It wasn't a long letter:

Trav,

I thought you should know before you come home that I'm with Ryan now.

~P

I wasn't surprised she broke it off clean like that. Paige has never been one for diplomacy. She usually says what's on her mind, even when it's hurtful or bitchy. Another thing I've always appreciated about her. Well, that . . . and the sex. Especially after we'd been fighting, which we did often. I still have a faint scar on my cheek from where she threw a beer bottle at me after she caught me making out with some random girl at some random party. We cheated on each other all the time. That's the way it was with me and Paige—insane and toxic, but always fucking awesome.

When I enlisted, I didn't pretend she'd sit at home waiting for me. I didn't tape her picture inside my helmet the way some of my buddies did with pictures of their wives and girlfriends. I always knew she'd hook up with someone else. The only surprising part was that the someone else was my brother.

The thing is? I don't *really* care.

I mean, yeah, I might be a little curious about why Paige would be interested in Ryan. He doesn't seem to be her type, which makes me wonder if she's playing some sort of mind game with me—or him. I have no interest in being played and I'm only in town for thirty days. Ryan can have her.

I didn't even want to come to Fort Myers, but I didn't have anywhere else to go. I'd rather be with my friends. I want to be with the people who know me best.

I want to go home.

As soon as the thought crystallizes in my mind, I feel bad again. Especially with my mom standing beside me at the baggage carousel, wearing the biggest smile in the history of smiles and rattling on about how happy she is I made it home before Ryan leaves for college. To keep from sniping a smart-ass comment about my level of give-a-shitness, I look around the room at the hugging families and business-men with laptop bags slung over their shoulders. Beyond a cluster of people waiting for their luggage, I see a dark-haired guy wearing desert camouflage leaning against a support col-umn. It looks like my buddy Charlie Sweeney. We've been friends since boot camp and were sent to Afghanistan in the same platoon.

"Charlie?" I take a step toward him and this weird sort of happiness fizzes up inside me like a soda bottle, because if my best friend is here in Florida, it means he's not—

"Travis?" my mom says. "Who are you talking to?"

—dead.

My stomach churns and my eyes go hot with tears that never seem to come. Charlie can't possibly be in Fort Myers because he was killed in Afghanistan and I'm standing in the middle of a crowded baggage claim talking out loud—to an empty space. And all that happy just leaks right out, leaving me empty again.

"Are you all right?" Mom touches my sleeve.

I blow out a breath and lie. "Yeah, I'm fine."

"I can't get over how you've changed," Mom says, hugging me again. I've always been tall, but I've grown two inches in the past year. Also, I used to have hair that hung nearly to my shoulders that Mom was always nagging me to cut. "You look so handsome."

The black-flapped opening spits my bag onto the conveyor and I'm relieved to walk away from this conversation. I grab the bag with one hand and hoist it onto my shoulder, sending little puffs of dust into the air around me. Afghanistan has followed me home.

"Welcome home, Marine." An old man approaches me, his sleeve pushed up to display the Marine Corps EGA—eagle, globe, and anchor—tattooed on his upper arm. Showing me he belongs to the brotherhood. "Semper Fi."

"Always, sir." I shake his hand.

He pats my elbow and lets me go. "God bless you, kid."

Mom chatters endlessly on the drive, mostly about school. She's the secretary at my former high school, so she thinks she knows all the gossip. I don't care who's dating who, or which teachers won't be hired back next year, or that the soccer team had a losing season, but letting her talk means I don't have to.

The house looks exactly the same as it did when I left, including Mom's ceramic frog next to the front steps. She keeps a spare key hidden underneath in case we get locked out. All my friends know the key is there, but Paige is the only one who's ever used it. She would drive over in the middle of the night and sneak up to my room. I wonder if she does that with Ryan now.

My mom leads me through the house to my bedroom, as if I don't remember the way. She opens the door and—like the rest of the house—it looks like it was frozen in time. Gray paint? Check. Color-coordinated comforter? Check. Concert flyers taped randomly to the walls to disguise the decorator paint job? Check. Curled-up photo of Paige and me at my senior prom stuck in the corner of the mirror? Check. Even the book on the bedside table is the same one I was reading before I left. The whole thing is . . . creepy.

"I left everything the way it was," she says as I drop my bag on the floor. "So it would feel familiar. Like home."

I don't tell her it doesn't feel like home at all. I pull the photo from the mirror, crush it in my fist, and lob it at the trash can.

"Why don't you rest?" Mom suggests. "Take a nap. I'll come get you when Dad and Rye are home."

When she's gone, I dive onto the bed. It's the one thing I'm very happy about. The mattress is soft and the comforter is clean, luxuries I've lived without since I left for boot camp. I stretch out on my back, my boots hanging off the bottom edge of the bed, and close my eyes. I can't get comfortable. I roll over onto my side and try again. Then my stomach. Pry off my boots with my toes. Finally, I grab my pillow and hit the floor, dragging the comforter with me. I've slept on the top bunk of a squeaky metal rack in the squad bay at Parris Island, on a cot at Camp Bastion while we waited to start our mission, and in February the temperature dropped so low one night I had to share a sleeping bag with Charlie. All things considered, the thick carpet is comfortable, and I fall asleep fast.

*　*　*

I'm walking down a road in Marjah. It's a road we've walked often on patrol. I'm on point with Charlie and Moss behind me. It's cold, clear, and quiet, except for the crunch of our boots and the sound of prayer we hear every morning. The street will come alive soon with people going to the mosque, washing in the canal, or going to work in their fields. Right now, though, the street is empty. The hair on the back of my neck prickles and I know something is going to go down. I stop and try to warn Moss and Charlie, but no sound comes out of my mouth. I try to signal with my hands, but I can't lift them. I want to run back to stop them, but my legs won't move no matter how hard I try. I watch, helpless, as Charlie steps on the pressure plate. Boom! He's enveloped in a cloud of dust. The bomb, hidden in the base of a tree, sprays him with shrapnel. Charlie falls to the dirt road, motionless. My limbs unfreeze and I walk slowly toward his body until I'm standing over him. The world shifts and I'm on my back, pain radiating through my body, as if I'd stepped on the mine, not Charlie. I open my eyes and there's a face above me. An Afghan boy I've seen before who smiles as he fades away.

* * *

I shoot upright on the floor, my eyes open and my body on alert, but my brain is still in the hazy space between nightmare and awake. My mother is shaking me. My hands curl around her wrists, squeezing until she cries out in pain. "Travis, stop!"

I let go immediately and just sit there, blinking, my heart rate going crazy. I'm shaking a little. Mom smoothes her hand across my forehead the way she did when I was small and had a fever. "It's only a dream. Let it go. It's not real."

I'm fully awake now and I know she's right. *It's not real.* This nightmare is a patchwork of my worst fears. But my imagination wraps itself in this quilt of horror whenever I sleep. I haven't averaged more than a couple hours a night for weeks.

As my heart rate drops back to normal, I watch her rub her wrists. I could have broken them. "I'm sorry I hurt you," I say. "I didn't mean to do that."

"It's okay." She looks at me sadly. "I wish I could erase whatever troubles your dreams."

Except the past can't be rewound and this is the life I chose.

*   *   *

I didn't have a noble purpose in joining the Marines. I didn't do it to protect American freedom and I wasn't inspired to action by the 9/11 terrorist attacks. I was in grade school then, and the biggest priority in my life was any bell that signaled it was time to leave school. I enlisted mostly because I wanted to escape my dad, who'd made my life hell since I quit the football team at the end of sophomore season.

I hated football. Not because I wasn't good at it or because it wasn't fun, but because I hated the way it took over my life. Dad signed me up for Pop Warner Tiny Mites when I was five. So while other kids were learning to ride two-wheelers, I was practicing my receiving. It was fun when I was little—the game was still a game—but as I got older, I hated the pressure. I hated that run-through-a-woodchipper feeling I got after he'd critique my game films. But what I hated most was that in practically every reference to me—in newspapers, game commentary, post-game TV recaps on the local news—was a reference to him. I was never just Travis Stephenson. I was *son of former Green Bay Packer Dean Stephenson*. Sophomore year he started talking about scouts and college ball, and all I could think about was how I was going to be stuck living my dad's dream. So when the season ended, I quit. He went ballistic, and I became a nonentity.

The day I turned eighteen—three days after I graduated high school—I went to the Marine recruiter's office and signed up. More or less. The process is more involved than simply signing your life over to the US Marine Corps, but the result is the same: four years of active duty, the next four years in ready reserve. It might not make sense to want to go from a lifetime of coaches yelling in my face to a drill instructor yelling in my face, but I figured it couldn't be that much different. Except that at boot camp I wouldn't be *son of former Green Bay Packer Dean Stephenson*. I'd just be me.

Mom cried when I told her because, in her mind, enlistment meant certain death in a foreign country. She begged me to enroll at Edison State instead. "I know you didn't get the best grades," she said. "But you can take the basics until you decide on a major. Please, Travis, don't do this."

My dad just looked at me for a long time, his mouth a tight slash across his face. It was a familiar expression. One reserved for me. In his world, where winning is everything, he had no use for the kid who refused to play the game. If I had picked up another sport, he might have forgiven me. But I didn't and neither did he.

His laugh was whip-crack sharp. "Remember the motorcycle you were going to rebuild? Or the band you and your friends were going to start? Or, wait—how about the promising football career you threw away like it was garbage instead of your God-given gift? How long, Travis, do you think you'll last at boot camp before you want to quit that, too? You don't have the discipline it takes to be a Marine."

As if he knew any more about being in the military than I did.

Three weeks later, I shipped and didn't come back. Until now.

I can admit now it might not have been one of my smarter decisions, but I didn't want to go to college and I didn't think I was going to end up in Afghanistan right out of infantry school. I figured I'd be assigned to a base or sent off to Okinawa. Thing is, I'm a good Marine. Better than pretty much anything else I've ever done. So even though the Marine Corps has moments of extreme suck, I don't really regret my choice.

"Trav." Mom taps at my bathroom door as I'm doing up the last button on a blue-and-white-striped shirt I found hanging in the closet. It's either Ryan's or something my mom bought before I left, hoping I'd wear it. The sleeves pinch at the elbows when I bend my arms, but I wore the same desert cammies for seven months. My fashion sense has atrophied. "Dinner in five minutes."

I wipe the steam from the mirror. I went for so long without seeing myself that my face still kind of surprises me. It feels like I'm looking at a stranger. Someone who is smaller than I imagined, although not small at all. And the guy in the mirror is not wearing a combat uniform or body armor. Without them, I don't feel much like myself, either.

The scent of roast beef greets me in the hallway, and I swear if Paige were standing naked in front of me, begging to get back together, I'd pass her by to get to the table. The closest we came to a home-cooked meal in-country was the time some of the Afghan National Army soldiers roasted a whole goat, which we ate with a local rice dish and Afghan bread. We had chicken from the village bazaar a couple of times, too, but mostly we ate MREs. Which is short for Meal, Ready-to-Eat. Or, as we usually called it, Meal, Rarely Edible.

"Travis." My dad gets up from the head of the table as I enter the dining room and shakes my hand, as if I'm a business associate. Or a stranger he hopes will buy a car. He's still wearing a suit, his yellow tie slack at the neck. "Welcome home, son."

"Yeah, thanks."

Mom prods Ryan, who is sitting across from me, texting someone on his cell phone. We're barely a year apart, but he looks so young.

"Hey, Trav." He smiles at the screen, then gives me a weak-ass chin lift. "Welcome back."

Jesus, this is awkward.

My family has never been especially good at warm and fuzzy. My mom's thing was always ferrying us to practices, supplying juice boxes at halftime, and sitting in the stands at every game. Even rainy days she'd be there, huddled under her green-and-white umbrella. Dad's displays of affection came after a win, accompanied by a manly pat on the shoulder and an *I'm proud of you, son*. It's been a long time since I got one of those. And Ryan . . . when I was seven and he was six, our grandpa gave me a Korean war G.I. Joe for my birthday. It was meant to be a collector's item, but Pops said I should play with it, enjoy it. Sometimes I did, but mostly I kept it on top of my dresser because I thought it was cool. One day, Ryan took it without asking. When I complained to my dad, he told me to quit whining and let my brother play with the G.I. Joe. Ryan pulled the arm off. That pretty much sums up our relationship: I have it. He wants it. He gets it. He ruins it.

Even so, shouldn't it feel good to be with them again? Why do I feel closer to a group of guys I've known less than a year than I do my own family?

"Did you get all the packages I sent?" Mom asks, passing me the serving dish of mashed potatoes.

After she accepted that I was going to enlist with or without her blessing, she pursued being a Marine Mom with the same enthusiasm as being a Football Mom. She registered on a bunch of Internet USMC parent websites, slapped a yellow magnetic *Support Our Troops* ribbon on her SUV, and went insane with care packages. Between church groups, the different "any service member" organizations, and parents, it wasn't unusual for a guy to get fifteen care packages at once. Getting mail was like Christmas, sitting there cross-legged on the ground opening presents. And my mom usually sent me quality stuff—instant heat packs, a coffee press and gourmet beans, and a solar shower that was stolen by one of the Afghan National Army soldiers before I even had a chance to use it.

"Yes, ma'am. Thank you." I was pretty terrible at keeping in touch, but in my defense, we were cut off from the outside world for the first couple of months we were there. Then we got a satellite phone and were allowed to call home every couple of weeks, but only for about five minutes at a time. During one call I suggested she could probably cut back on the dental floss and paperback mysteries and send some school supplies for the kids who would mob us, begging for *everything*. "The kids went nuts for the pens and crayons." Water. Candy. Food. Pens. I don't know why, but they loved pens. "I'm, um—sorry I didn't call much."

Her eyes widen. Probably because I've never been in the habit of apologizing.

"Well, we figured you were probably busy," she says.

In Afghanistan, that was true, but I have no excuse for

boot camp or infantry school. She sent me tons of letters and I never answered any of them. I called her on the first day of boot camp and recited the words fastened to the wall beside the phone: *This is recruit Stephenson. I have arrived safely at Parris Island. Please do not send any food or bulky items to me in the mail. I will contact you in three to five days by postcard with my new address. Thank you for your support.* And that was about it. Aside from that handful of five-minute phone calls, I haven't talked to her for more than a year.

"Ellen always called me after she got a letter from Charlie," Mom says. "So I knew you were okay."

At boot camp we did everything in alphabetical order, so the two other recruits whose names I learned first were Lee Staples and Charlie Sweeney. One of them was always in front of me or behind me, depending on the whim of our drill instructors. Staples bugged me because he cried after we got our heads shaved. I mean, okay, I can see how it could be considered degrading because it strips away one of the things that sets you apart from everyone else, but what-the-fuck-ever. It grows back. Anyway, when they finally let us get to sleep that first day, after being awake more than twenty-four hours straight, Charlie and I were assigned to the same rack—Stephenson on the top bunk, Sweeney on the bottom. We were stripping down to shorts and T-shirts when Charlie said, "Hey, Stephenson, I heard if you go to the Buddhist church services on Sundays, they let you sleep."

"I heard," I said. "If you claim to be Jewish, you can go to Sabbath services and still have time off on Sunday."

Charlie laughed. "I like the way you think."

I'm not going to tell you I knew right then we were going to be friends, but he wasn't a whiner like Staples. I don't know why it was Charlie who became my best friend. It's not one particular reason I can identify. I had his back. He had mine. Period. Somehow I guess Charlie's mom and mine became friends, too.

"We're so proud of you." Mom's eyes get watery and my dad nods in agreement, which makes me wonder if the Four Horsemen of the Apocalypse can be far behind.

"So what was it like over there?" Dad's eyes glow with something I haven't seen in years. At least not while he was looking at me. "Did you kill anybody?"

He's curious. Who wouldn't be? But how do I answer that question? Yes, I've killed, but it's not like picking off bad guys in a video game. The first time I shot someone, I thought I was going to puke, but I couldn't because we were in the middle of a firefight and I couldn't stop shooting. I won't tell my dad that. Not at dinner. Not ever.

"I don't really want to talk about it," I say.

His pride fades as his eyes narrow. "Why? Do you think you're too good—"

"Travis, did I tell you?" Mom interrupts him. "There's an organization in Tampa that's been collecting school supplies for the kids—"

"I'm sure he doesn't want to hear about your little pet project, Linda," Dad cuts in. I'm surprised to hear him talk this way to my mom. No matter how bad things got between him and me, he's always been good to her.

"No, Dad," I say. "I don't think I'm too good to tell you about Afghanistan. I just don't want to talk about killing people at the fucking dinner table." Not waiting for his response, I turn to Mom. "And I *do* want to hear about your project."

Her eyes flicker nervously toward my dad. He makes a wide-armed shrug and rolls his eyes. His Super Bowl ring flashes on his hand, a huge reminder that he is a Winner.

"I was just—" Mom stumbles over the words, the light gone from her eyes. "I was just going to say that I've talked to them about starting a branch here in Fort Myers."

"That's really cool." I smile at her. The begging kids were okay at first because they were scared of us, but after a while they were grabby and demanding. I don't tell her that, though. She seems pretty excited. "The kids go crazy for that stuff. Pens, paper, soccer balls, and those beanbag animal dolls— they lose their minds over those things."

"May I be excused?" Ryan balls up his napkin and drops it on his plate. "I've got a, um . . ." His gaze meets mine for a split second before sliding nervously away. A date. He has a date with Paige. "I'm meeting up with some people."

"Maybe Travis would like to go along," Mom suggests.

"I'll pass." The image of me riding shotgun with my

brother and my ex-girlfriend almost makes me laugh. "I'm wiped out."

Ryan shoves away from the table and the three of us spend the rest of the meal in a silence thick with things unsaid. The only sound is the clinking of silverware against the plates. I hate that a year wasn't enough separation to keep my dad from getting under my skin, and I hate that I let him make me feel fifteen all over again. When it's finally over, I go to my room and lock the door.

We got back to Camp Lejeune a couple of weeks ago and had to have a post-deployment health assessment to take care of any physical problems we developed in-country— primarily skin problems from washing in muddy canals, acne from having a constantly dirty face, bug bites, and a few guys had lingering coughs from chest infections. The evaluation is also supposed to gauge our mental wellness, but that's a joke. We say everything is okay because the fastest way to wreck your career is to admit it's not. So I didn't tell anyone about my recurring nightmare. I only told the doctor I was having trouble sleeping and he prescribed me some pills.

They rattle as I pull the amber bottle out of my bag and dump three tablets into my hand. I swallow them dry, then ease myself to the floor and let the world fade away.

Chapter 2

A loud bang jolts me awake and I reach for my rifle. For a couple of seconds I panic because it's gone, then I remember I'm in Florida and my rifle is in the armory in North Carolina.

"Travis! Travis!" My mom is pounding on the door and she sounds frantic. I unlock it and she launches herself at me, nearly strangling me in the process. "Oh, thank God. You're awake."

Something wet trickles down my bare chest. She's crying. "Mom, what's wrong?"

"You've been asleep for sixteen hours." She catches a shuddering breath. "And your door was locked. I thought—I was afraid you overdosed."

There are moments—thousands of them during the course of every single day—when I'm swamped with guilt that I came home alive and Charlie didn't, but I don't have a death wish. I scrub my eye with the heel of my hand, dislodging sixteen hours' worth of crust. "I was just exhausted." I pat her awkwardly on the back. "I haven't had a good night's sleep in a while. I didn't mean to scare you."

Wiping her tears on the back of her hand, she surveys the nest of blankets on the floor. "Is something wrong with your bed?"

"I've spent a lot of time sleeping on the ground." There were nights we slept in holes in the ground. Other nights, we slept in abandoned compounds. Our patrol base was an abandoned schoolhouse with holes in the roof and birds in residence in the ceiling. "I'm not quite used to a bed yet."

She sits down on my bed. "Do you want a firmer mattress or— What happened to your legs?"

"They're, um . . ." I look down at the fading red welts that circle my ankles and creep up my calves. "They're flea bites."

"Flea bites?" She looks horrified.

"Yeah, well, after a while everything gets really dirty," I explain. "And the people over there have mud-walled courtyards around their houses where they keep their livestock. Sometimes we'd sleep in there."

Charlie's mom sent him a flea collar once that he strapped

around his ankle, but it didn't work. We called him Fido for a while after that, but he'd just bark and go, "Devil dog! Oorah!" which would crack us up every time.

"You slept with—" Her hand comes up to her mouth. "I can't—I don't even know what to say." Her eyes fill again.

Afghanistan sucked. In the summer we sweated our balls off in the hot sun. In the winter we had to battle hypothermia. It was the coldest I've ever been in my life, even colder than when we lived in Green Bay. Poisonous snakes. Scorpions. Flies. Fleas. Sandstorms. Knowing that every time we left our patrol base, someone was going to shoot at us. I don't miss it exactly, but it feels as if I'll never be fully at home here again. "It wasn't so bad."

* * *

"There's a party tonight at the Manor." Ryan pokes his head into my room after another uncomfortable family dinner of awkward small talk and things left unsaid. I'm unpacking my bag. The dresser drawers, I discover, are empty—apparently Mom didn't keep everything the same. Before, she was always nagging me to dress nicer and was embarrassed that I bought clothes at the Salvation Army. She probably had a field day throwing away all my ratty T-shirts and jeans with holes. Doesn't matter. None of them would have fit.

"You interested?" Ryan asks.

The Manor is a dilapidated rental house on the beach

that's part commune, part concert venue. My friend Eddie Ramos has been living there since graduation, but we've been partying there since we were freshmen. I'm not sure I'm ready to see my old friends yet, but I don't want to spend the evening watching military crime shows with my parents. Not only because it's always a Marine who ends up dead on those shows, but because I can't take another uncomfortable minute in their silence. I don't know what's going on with them. I always thought they were solid. "Yeah, sure."

Ryan dangles the car keys from his fingers. "Wanna drive?"

I snatch them. "Meet you at the car."

Outside, I lower myself into the driver's seat of the red VW Corrado that used to be mine and run my hands along the steering wheel. The faint scent of pot mixed with McDonald's brings back memories of all the hours I spent with this car—working on it, driving aimlessly around Fort Myers with friends, messing around with Paige in the backseat. I found the car on the Internet when I was fifteen and bought it with my own money. Did all of the work on it, too. It bothers me a little that Ryan felt entitled to appropriate the car after I left, but I've never said anything. I wasn't using it. Now . . . it doesn't really feel like mine anymore.

Ryan drops into the passenger seat and the scent of cologne overwhelms the car. I cough and roll down my window. "Damn, Rye, did you bathe in that shit?"

"Paige likes it," he says. "She bought it for my birthday."

My eyebrows hitch up. "She did?"

He nods and when he gives me a cocky grin, I see the chip in his front tooth from the time he wiped out at the skate-park. There's so much wrong with this conversation, I don't know where to begin. Paige hated when I smelled like anything but me.

If Kenny "Kevlar" Chestnut were here right now, he'd theorize in his Tennessee drawl that chicks are naturally attracted to the scent of badass. He's a wiry little guy with bright red hair and a lower lip constantly bulging with Skoal. We call him Kevlar because he's the only one in our squad who could stomach the pork rib MRE, so we figure his stomach must be lined with Kevlar. He talks real fast, as if he doesn't get all the words out at once, they'll disappear. He talks shit about girls, even though he has zero experience and even less game. Charlie never let him get away with it.

"I call bullshit, Kenneth," he said once, after Kevlar claimed he had sex with a University of Tennessee cheer-leader. "You're just a red-haired little bast—"

"Shut the fuck up." Kevlar gets all huffy when we make fun of his hair or call attention to the fact that he is the small-est guy in our platoon. "Solo's got red hair, too." Mine is closer to brown than red, but he thinks including me in his affliction will lend him credibility.

I laughed and dropped my arm around his shoulder. "The color of your hair is irrelevant when you're as hand-some as me."

The memory brings both happiness and pain. I squeeze my eyes shut and inhale a deep breath.

"You okay, bro?" Ryan brings me back to the moment. "This whole thing with Paige isn't—"

"Messed up?" I look over at him, with his shaggy hair and the shell necklace he wears because he thinks it makes him look like a surfer, and his face is as earnest as I've ever seen it. He really likes her. "Completely, but—" I cut a cross in the air the way the priest does at church, and start the engine. "You have my blessing."

We haven't even gotten out of our development when I notice a lot of play in the clutch as I shift from gear to gear.

"How long has the clutch been like this?" I ask.

"Like what?" Ryan says.

"Burned out."

"It seemed okay to me."

I let out the clutch and the car stutters as it accelerates. "*Okay?* You work at a fucking VW dealership."

"I'm not a mechanic."

"You don't have to be a mechanic to know when your clutch is messed up." I'm probably angrier than I should be. I know how to replace a burned-out clutch, but it's the principle of the thing. There was nothing wrong with the car when I left. This is classic Ryan. And my car is Korean war G.I. Joe.

He doesn't apologize. He doesn't say anything at all. He

just looks all butthurt—like I'm the bad guy—and then turns his face toward the window.

* * *

As we head toward the beach I notice the differences in the landscape of the city. New businesses that weren't there last year. Old businesses that are gone. It's like a whole chunk of time has just . . . disappeared. The songs on the radio are different. The faces on the celebrity tabloids at the airport newsstand were people I didn't recognize. There's even a new American fucking Idol.

We pull up in front of the Manor, and I guess I'm expecting it to be different, too. Except the white cottage with the crooked porch steps never changes. There's a beer can on the porch railing that's been sitting there as long as I can remember. Even on the rare occasion someone decides to clean the place, no one ever touches the beer can. It's become art.

"Trav, dude, where you been?" The first person to greet me is Cooper Middleton, half-baked and heavy-lidded, a halo of pot smoke around his dirty blond head. He's sitting in the same saggy lawn chair he was sitting in the last time I was there. Maybe he's been there the whole time. With Cooper, it's not implausible. He graduated with me, but as far as I know he's never had a job—unless selling weed counts.

"Afghanistan."

He looks off into the middle distance for a moment, a ghost of a smile on his face, and I can tell he's somewhere else. "Oh, yeah . . . sweet."

The living room is a mosh pit, all the thrift store furniture pushed up against the walls to make room for dancing, and a band—made up of some of the people who live at the Manor—warms up in the dining room. As I walk through the house, people reach out to me, shaking my hand and welcoming me home. Instead of feeling welcome, I feel hemmed in, like at the airport. Jittery. Freaked out at being in the middle of a crowd without my rifle.

"I need a beer," I say to no one, and my trigger finger flexes as I press my way through the crowd to the kitchen. Paige is perched on the counter, a plastic cup and cigarette in the same hand, gesturing widely as she talks to a group of girls. Paige has an opinion about everything and sometimes she will not shut up. But her black hair is marble shiny and her plush lips are stained red from whatever she's drinking, so who cares what she's saying? Her eyes break away from her friends and meet mine. I feel the magnetic pull and have to remind myself she's not mine anymore.

Before I can approach her, Eddie comes up. "Trav, man, welcome home!"

He goes in for a slap hug that I know will turn into a takedown attempt. It always does. He lowers his shoulder and circles my waist with his arms, trying to wrestle me to the floor. We used to be more evenly matched, but now he doesn't stand a chance. I curl my leg around his and drop him.

"Dude, you may as well call terminal uncle." I laugh as I haul him to his feet.

"It's been too fucking long." He gives me a hug for real this time. "How ya been?"

"Good." Lie. "You?"

"Same shit, different day, you know?" Eddie shrugs.

I have no idea what it's like to be the nineteen-year-old night manager of Taco Bell with a pregnant girlfriend. I'm not saying Eddie made the wrong choices—he's living an honest life and it's not my place to judge—but, no, I *don't* know. I've spent the better part of a year on the other side of the planet in a country where a guy will shake your hand and smile, then go pick up his AK-47 and shoot at you. Where a little boy will demand—with no tears in his eyes— that you give him a hundred bucks' compensation for acci- dentally killing his mother, which is less than the going rate for killing his dog.

Paige hops down from the counter and walks toward me and my brother. I can see her red string bikini through the thin white tank top she's wearing. I've unstrung that bikini before. She goes to Ryan first—so weird—reaching up on tiptoe to ruffle his hair as she kisses him. His arm slips around her waist. Her face is different when she looks up at him. Softer. Less angry. "You smell good."

Ryan doesn't look at me, but I see the I-told-you-so-grin tug at his lips. I laugh. Paige cocks her head at me and smiles. "Well, if it isn't G.I. Joe."

"G.I. Joe"—I take her drink and down it in a single swallow. It's fruity, but the alcohol is strong—"was a pussy."

She laughs her smoky, sexy laugh and kisses my cheek, her boobs—which her parents bought for her fifteenth birthday—brushing against my arm. "Welcome home."

"Thanks for the care package," I say. "Miss January brought a lot of guys a lot of pleasure." She laughs again.

"It was the least I could do."

"How's Bill?" I ask.

Her dad owns a national barricade company that supplies orange barrels, cement barricades, and traffic cones to construction jobs. Every single barricade has his name on it. He and Paige's mom never liked me.

She shrugs. "Still hates you."

"Figures."

"So how long are you home, Trav?" Eddie asks.

"A month," I say.

He nods. "Nice."

The noise of the party fills in the space where the conversation should continue but doesn't, and Eddie just does that nervous little laugh people do when they don't know what to say. This never happened with Charlie. We talked about everything, from the philosophical to the ridiculous—like who would win in a fight between a liger and a grizzly/polar bear hybrid. We nearly got into a fight ourselves over that one.

"How's, um—how's Jenn?" I ask.

"She's good." He nods again. "The baby is due in September. A girl."

"That's awesome, man, congratulations." I take a sip of beer, looking for an escape. Eddie was my best friend in high school, but now . . . I know there's a place inside me that still cares about him—about all of them—but tonight I can't really find it.

The band starts playing, and Eddie looks relieved. Maybe we were both looking for an escape. "Talk to you later, bro?"

I nod and he's swallowed up by the dancing mass of people in the living room. The bass makes the walls rattle and I wonder if this will be one of those nights when the neighbors call the police. In the middle of the crowd I see one dark head, standing still in the middle of the thrashing bodies. Black hair spikes out from his head in random cowlicks like . . . Charlie.

He stares at me.

I blink, and he's gone.

"Travis, are you okay?" I hear Ryan's voice pulling me back to reality. "You spaced out for a second."

"Yeah, I'm fine." But I'm not. Sweat trickles between my shoulder blades beneath my shirt. "I just need a beer."

Cooper is at the keg, refilling his cup. "Trav, my man! Where you been?"

Kid seriously needs to cut back on the weed. "We've already had this conversation, Coop."

"Oh, yeah." A stoned giggle rolls out of him. "Afghanistan, right?"

"Right."

"Dude, did you see any poppies?"

Leave it to Cooper to ask me about the drugs. "Like the *Wizard of Oz*, man," I say, because that will make him happy, but we didn't take naps in the poppy fields of Afghanistan. We took fire from the Taliban.

I fill a cup, then go out to the living room, my insides still coiled from—I'm not even sure what to call what happened. Hallucination? Haunting?

Standing with my back to the wall, I watch the party going on around me. A couple of girls in tiny skirts stare at me on their way upstairs to the bathroom. Derek Michalski, who graduated with the unofficial senior superlative of Most Likely to Do Time for Dating Underage Girls, is hitting on a girl who looks about twelve or thirteen. Cooper and his girl, April, are deep into one of those stoned conversations filled with profound insights they won't remember tomorrow. Used to be I was part of this. Now I wonder where, if anywhere, I fit. And if I even care.

A few beers later, I return to the kitchen, where Eddie,

Paige, Ryan, and a few others are sitting around the table, reminiscing about some road trip they took last summer. Paige is sitting on Ryan's knee, his hand curled around her hip. She plays with his hair as she talks over Eddie to be heard. ". . . and then the fucking car died in the middle of nowhere, remember? And . . ."

I sit for a while, but I'm not really paying attention. I'm thinking about the last time I got drunk. Just before we deployed, Kevlar smuggled a bottle of cheap, nasty tequila into our room and we drank it while watching *M*A*S*H* episodes on Charlie's old TV. When Kevlar passed out, snoring and drooling on my pillow, Charlie told me that back home in St. Augustine he lived with his mom and her lesbian partner, and that his dad was an anonymous donor.

"I don't really talk about it because I don't want to get shit for it, you know?" he said. "Charlie has two mommies. Shit like that." I might have made fun of him if I hadn't been so drunk, but the tequila made us maudlin. Morbid. "If anything happens to me over there, Solo, I want you to go see her, okay?"

"Dude, don't be so fucking stupid," I said. "I'm never going to meet your mom because the only thing that's ever going to happen to you is me, kicking your ass."

I was wrong. The worst thing did happen—and I couldn't stop it.

I lift my beer cup for a drink. Dirt fills the lines of my hand, and my fingers are stained with blood. The cup slips from my grasp, splashing beer across the top of the table. Paige jumps off Ryan's lap, shrieking something at me, but I don't understand what she's saying. My chest is tight and I'm having trouble breathing.

I have to get out of here.

My chair falls over as I stand up.

"Trav, where are you going?" Ryan calls after me, but I don't answer. I push my way through the living room and out the front door. The air is cooler outside, clear, as I pull it into my lungs in giant gasps until my heart rate returns to its regular rhythm. I look at my hands. They're clean.

I walk down the street toward the Shamrock, the biker bar on the corner of Delmar and Estero. Apart from bikers, the only people who go there are leather-skinned old beach rats and brittle-haired women who think they're still young and hot. The music is dirtball rock, the floor is sticky, and the beer is served in plastic cups, but they're good about looking the other way when you "forget" your ID.

Going through the open doorway, I pass Gage Darnell. He was a year ahead of me at school, but dropped out when he turned eighteen. He's leaving with a familiar-looking girl with a fake tan, fake nails, fake blond hair, and probably fake boobs. She looks like an Internet porn star—and not necessarily in a good way. I went to school with her, too, but her name escapes me. Angel? Amber? Something strip clubby, I think.

"Hey, Travis, welcome home." Gage offers his fist to

bump, then continues on his way. The blonde wiggles her fingers at me, then latches on to his arm. I might have slept with her.

Perched on barstools are a couple more girls around my age. The one wearing cutoff shorts and cowboy boots is Lacey Ellison. She's not especially hot and wears too much makeup, but we didn't call her Easy-E in high school for nothing. She's flirting with a biker sporting a Hells Angels emblem on his leather vest and a dirty blond goatee. Lacey giggles at something he says and touches the snake tattoo on his forearm.

Beside her is a girl with a mass of light brown hair pulled into one of those sexy-messy knots. Compared to Lacey she's overdressed; the only skin showing is a narrow stripe between the top of her threadbare Levi's and a washed-out blue T-shirt. She doesn't acknowledge me—not even a little chin lift—as I claim the empty stool next to her and order a beer, and for some reason, this bothers me. Probably because I'm drunk. "Nice night, huh?"

Her green eyes meet mine in the Guinness mirror behind the bar and it feels like all the air has been sucked out of the room. I've never slept with this girl, but she was the first I remember wanting.

Harper Gray.

The first time I kissed her was at a middle school slumber party Paige threw when her parents went to Key West, leaving her alone for the weekend. It was at the end of summer and I was new, because my dad had just been traded to Tampa Bay, but I'd already made friends with most of the guys on the eighth-grade football team at early practice. The lure of alcohol and girls wearing pajamas was too strong to resist, so we crashed the party. After raiding the liquor cabinet, Paige decided it was time to play seven minutes in heaven. I went first, using the spinner from an old board game, and it landed on Harper.

"Your seven minutes start . . . now," Paige said as Harper followed me into the laundry room. I shut the door and she leaned against the washing machine, looking scared. I remember the sharp scent of the bleach mixed with the fabric smell of clean laundry. "I'm Travis."

"I know." Her eyes flicked shyly down to our feet—we were both wearing beat-up old Chucks and it seemed like a sign—then up at me. "I'm Harper."

I already knew, too.

"Like Harper Lee?" I was showing off. I hadn't read *To Kill a Mockingbird*, but it was on my mom's bookshelf, so I knew the author's name.

"No," she said. "Charley Harper."

"Oh, um . . ."

"He's an artist."

"Cool." My scope of small talk completely played out, I decided to go in for the kiss. Our noses bumped the first time and I could hear the shaky nervousness in her laugh. The second time we got it right, but I forgot to take the sour apple gum out of my mouth, so my tongue was all over the place as I tried to kiss her and hide the gum at the same time. It started out sloppy and ridiculous, but eventually we got it right and I remember my fingers sliding through the waves of her hair.

Nothing else happened. We just stood there, pressed against each other, kissing. Until Paige's voice told us our time was up. I didn't want to stop and was about to suggest we drop out of the game, when the door flew open. Paige grabbed Harper by the wrist and pulled her back out to the party.

She was tangled in a whispering knot of girls when I came out of the laundry room. All my friends wanted the details of what happened between me and Harper. They expected something good, so I embellished. Said she let me feel her up. By Monday, my lie had taken on a life of its own. People were saying Harper had sex with all the guys who crashed Paige's party. Calling her a slut. I don't know how it got so out of control, and I could have told everyone what really happened, but I didn't. When she came up to me in the cafeteria, I ignored her. By the following weekend, Paige was my girlfriend.

"Hey, Charley Harper, can I buy you a beer?" It's not the smoothest opening line I've ever used, but I'm not feeling smooth. I'm jagged. And drunk.

She lifts her nearly full cup but won't look at me. "Got one, thanks."

Okay.

"You might not remember me, but—"

"Travis Stephenson," she interrupts, her words like a roadblock. "Welcome home. Now leave me alone."

Damn, she's hostile.

"What's your problem?"

Harper stares at me a moment and I'm mesmerized by the green of her eyes. So I don't see it coming when she punches me in the face. "Are you *kidding* me?"

"Jesus Christ—ow!" My eye socket throbs—she definitely doesn't hit like a girl—and I'm going to have a black eye. "What was that for?"

"I was thirteen years old, Travis!" Harper is yelling at me and everyone is staring, including Lacey and her dirty biker. "I still played with Barbie dolls in secret when my friends weren't around. I didn't have sex with *anyone* at Paige's party, but you told everyone I did. And when I tried to deny it, no one believed me. You trashed my reputation and now I'm supposed to think it's cute you remembered I'm not named for Harper fucking Lee?"

"I didn't—"

"You didn't what? Didn't do it? Didn't mean it? Save the excuses."

I want to defend myself, but this moment is a lot like boot camp. It doesn't matter if I'm guilty or not. She's spent years believing I'm an asshole and the only thing that is going to fix it is an apology. "Harper—"

The bartender comes over. "Everything okay here?"

"Just fine," Harper snaps. "I'm leaving. You can put my beer on *his* tab."

Jesus, that was a cool move. And although she hates my guts, I'm kind of turned on and I wish she weren't leaving. "Add a shot of tequila, too," I tell the bartender, but he shakes his head. "You're done."

Which sucks, because I'm not nearly drunk enough. I down the rest of my beer and drop a pile of bills on the bar, hoping it's enough to make up for the drama I've caused here tonight. I turn to leave and Paige is standing there, her mouth all smug. I hate how she does that.

"Rye's looking for you," she says. "He's ready to go."

"Okay." My eyes wander down to her ass as I follow her out of the bar. Force of habit, I guess. Also, it's nice. Kind of bubbly.

"So, Harper Gray, huh?" she asks as we walk up the middle of the street.

"When it's your business, I'll let you know."

She snorts a laugh. "You can do so much better than her, Trav. She's beach trash."

"Shut up."

"Do you want me to come over later?" she asks.

"For what?"

She catches her full lower lip between her teeth and looks up at me from under her dark lashes. It's an innocent act that used to get me hot. I have to admit, it still works. "I think you know."

"So let me get this straight," I say. "You hook up with my brother behind my back and now you want me to do the same to him?"

She flicks her ice-blue eyes toward the night sky. "It's not like it means anything."

Somewhere in the recesses of my beer-soaked consciousness, I think this is meant to hurt me, but it doesn't. When I think about what Paige and I have had, love has never entered into it. "That's so messed up. You know that, right?"

"Do you want me to come over or not?"

"No."

"I'll be there at three."

* * *

Even before I open my eyes I can feel the presence of another person in my room, and the hair on the back of my neck puts my body on alert. Hand-to-hand combat is not usually the Taliban's style. They'd rather take our money at the local bazaar and use it to buy weapons to kill us. They prefer ambushes, roadside bombs, and sniping from windows and rooftops. But there is someone here with me in the dark and I'm not going to wait to be killed.

I surge upward, grabbing the intruder around the knees, and drop him to the floor. I pin him beneath me, the tip of my knife at his throat. In the slashes of moonlight coming through the blinds, I realize he is not a he. It's Paige. And for the first time since I've known her, she looks scared.

"Oh, shit!" I drop the knife as if it's red-hot and scrabble backward against the side of my bed. "Jesus, Paige, what the fu— Did I hurt you?"

Her fear falls away as she registers my surprise and she laughs as she picks up the knife. "You've always liked it a little rough, Trav, but this is extreme, don't you think?" She crawls toward me, the knife gripped in her hand, and straddles my lap. "But . . ." Her lips are so close to mine I can taste her breath. "I think I like it."

I take the knife from her and put it on the bedside table, on top of the book I'll never finish. She slides her tank top off.

"What are you doing here?" I ask.

"That"—she fishes a condom from the pocket of her tiny denim skirt—"should be obvious."

She unties her red bikini. This is so not something I should be doing, but her skin is warm and familiar and . . . here.

It's been a long time since I've gotten laid, but I've been living in the middle of a desert, where women are hidden under burqas. Besides, Muslim women . . . well, the Qur'an forbids nearly everything fun anyway, so even if you could see their faces, there's not much point in even considering it.

I did kiss a Muslim girl once. When Charlie and I arrived at Camp Lejeune, the rest of our unit was on pre-deployment leave. We had to stay on base for a crash-course version of all the training the battalion had done while we were still at infantry school. Just before we were scheduled to deploy, Charlie and I were given a few days' leave so we could go home. Instead, we went to New York City. Kevlar—we didn't even really know him very well, but he was new like Charlie and me—invited himself along.

At a club the first night, Charlie was hitting on this girl from Smith College. She told me her roommate had just broken up with her boyfriend and a kiss from a hot—her word, not mine—Marine would restore her friend's faith that not all men are assholes. As Charlie's wingman, I knew there was a better than average chance her friend was a dog, but I was committed and drunk.

Except she wasn't ugly. She was beautiful, with dark, hopeful eyes—even though she was trying not to look hopeful—and I couldn't have been an asshole if I wanted to. She wouldn't let me do anything other than kiss her—believe me, I tried—but the gods of getting laid smiled on me for the rest of the weekend. Afterward, Kevlar—who failed to seal the deal with every girl he met—called me a haji-lover for kissing a Muslim girl. He spent the trip to Afghanistan nursing a busted bottom lip.

When it's over, Paige moves off me and falls back against the bed, gasping for air. My own breath is short and my bones feel liquid. "Jesus, Trav, I forgot how fucking good it is with you."

She's right. It is good. Except when the adrenaline starts wearing off, I hate her. I hate my brother, too. Mostly I hate myself. "You need to go."

"Why?" She nuzzles my neck, as if we're still together.

"You got what you came for."

"Don't be that way." She reties her bikini. "You wanted it, too."

I shrug. "Fine. Stick around. You and your boyfriend can have breakfast together in a couple of hours."

Paige laughs. "You're jealous. How cute."

"I'm not."

Thing is, I'm really not. If I feel anything at all, it's anger— that she hasn't changed and that all the years we were together were a huge waste of time.

Chapter 3

I'm standing on the cracked sidewalk in front of a tiny orange-and-white cottage on Ohio Avenue, wondering what I'm going to do next, when a man comes out the front door. It's still dark, so at first I don't think he sees me.

"Is there a good reason why you're outside my house at four thirty in the morning?" he asks, resting a travel mug of coffee on the hood of an ancient Land Rover. His keys jingle as he unlocks the driver's-side door. He surveys my T-shirt, soaked through with sweat under the arms and in the middle of my chest. It's a long run from my house to Fort Myers Beach—and there's a bridge involved.

A little self-loathing goes a long way.

"Just ended up here, sir." I don't have a good answer. After Paige left, I pulled on my running shoes and took off.

I didn't even bring my cell phone. "Wasn't sure where else to go."

"Interesting choice of destinations."

I nod. "Not real well thought out, either."

He chuckles. "Need a lift somewhere?"

"I could use a ride home."

The porch light flickers to life and Harper steps out, the wooden screen door slapping shut behind her. "Travis?"

Her feet are bare and she's wearing little pajama shorts that sit low on her hips and make her mile-long legs go on forever. I have to look away. The last thing I need is to get a boner in front of her dad. "Yeah, um—hi."

Her dad's eyebrows lift, but he sips his coffee without comment.

"What are you doing here?" She steps off the porch into the small patch of sandy grass, sounding only marginally less annoyed with me than she was earlier. "Haven't you had enough abuse for one night?"

Apparently not. "I couldn't sleep, so I decided to get some air."

"You look like hell," she says. "Did you run the whole way?"

"More or less."

Her mouth falls open. "That has to be at least—"

"Seven miles." They both stare at me, but seven miles is nothing. What's more interesting is that she knows where I live.

"Well, o-kay." Harper's dad glances at his watch. "I need to get to work, so why don't you drop me off and then take Travis on home?"

"Let me go change real quick," she says.

Bummer. I kinda liked the pajamas.

"Nice Rover, sir." The Land Rover is older than me and except for a CD changer he probably installed himself, there are no creature comforts inside. The windows are crank-operated, the door locks are not automatic, and the spare tire is mounted in the middle of the hood.

"Thanks." The driver's door creaks as he slams it shut. "I bought her when I was in college. Every couple of months I need to replace a part or fix something, but she's a tough old girl."

"If you ever need a hand . . ." I stop, feeling like a moron and sounding like a suck-up.

"You know your way around an engine?"

"Some."

He nods. "You're Linda Stephenson's boy, aren't you?"

"Yes, sir." It's interesting that he mentions my mom and not my dad. Like maybe there's another person in this town who doesn't think the sun rises and sets on *former Green Bay Packer Dean Stephenson.*

"You can call me Bryan instead of sir," he says. "It makes me feel old."

"Yes, si—" Old habits die hard. "Okay."

"You used to be such a little douchebag." He's one of

those older guys who can use a term like "douchebag" without sounding like one. The same way he can get away with wearing a Meat Puppets T-shirt and not look as if he's trying too hard. Anyway, given that the last two things I did tonight were get punched by his daughter and have sex with my brother's girlfriend, I'm pretty sure I still qualify as a douchebag.

"Yep. I sure was."

Harper reemerges from the house, this time wearing the same jeans and blue T-shirt she was wearing at the bar. As she climbs into the backseat, I turn around to look at her and notice Elvis Costello's face on the front of her shirt. So cool.

"Hey, I forgot to tell you last night," Harper's dad says, glancing briefly in the rearview mirror at her as he backs out of the driveway. "But I reconnected online with an old college friend of mine. She's thinking of coming for a visit."

Harper rolls her eyes. "My dad discovered Facebook."

"What do you do that you have to be at work so early?" I ask him.

"I do the morning show at Z88."

"Wait. You're Bryan of Bryan and Joe's Morning Z?"

"Yeah," he says.

"I used to make my roommates listen to your show on the Internet."

He laughs. "And they still speak to you?"

"Are you kidding? They loved it. You should be syndicated."

The Morning Z is the perfect show because they don't pretend to know everything when they're talking about stuff, their guests aren't lame, and they play more music. Everyone I know listens to that show.

"We've talked about it," he says. "But that brings pressure we aren't sure we want." He glances at me. "You know, if you ever wanted to come talk about Afghanistan . . ."

I imagine telling all of southwest Florida how Kevlar used to jack off to a picture of Wonder Woman—the cartoon, not Lynda Carter. The thought makes me chuckle. "I'll think about it."

A few minutes later, we're at the radio station. Bryan invites me in for a tour, but I turn him down. It's been a long, strange night and I feel like I might be tired enough to sleep without pills. "I should probably get home."

He disappears inside the building and Harper takes over the driving. "Are you hungry?" she asks, turning onto Daniels in a direction opposite from the way to my house.

This is not a question I expected. I'm not especially hungry. I'm exhausted and I can still smell Paige on my skin. Except I think Harper is asking me to spend more time with her. This might make me a glutton for punishment, but I don't want to refuse. "Starved."

She pulls into the Waffle House out by I-75 and we sit in a booth by the windows. After ordering a couple of All-Star breakfasts with eggs over easy and bacon, Harper looks at me. "Why are you here?"

I stir my black coffee with a spoon, just to do something with my hands. "I guess I wanted to apologize. I was stupid when I was fourteen, and clearly I haven't made much progress since."

"Do you think an apology is enough?" she asks. "Do you know how many guys grab my butt or say disgusting things to me because they think I'm the kind of girl who enjoys that? I've never had a boyfriend. I've never been to the prom. I've never even been out on a real date."

"I'm sorry."

"Paige . . ." She blows out a sharp breath, as if even saying the name is an effort. Paige has that effect on a lot of people. "Paige Manning slept her way through the senior class, including your brother, while you were gone, and *I'm* considered a slut. But do you want to hear the best part?"

I don't. I feel bad enough as it is. Harper leans across the table, her face only a few inches from mine. Close enough I can see the sun freckles scattered on her cheeks and nose. Close enough that if I thought I could get away with kissing her without getting punched again, I probably would. "I've never slept with anyone. Ever."

"I'm—"

"I know." She falls back against her side of the booth, her eyes locked on mine. "You're sorry."

The waitress slides our plates onto the table and Harper looks away. Silently, I dig into my hash browns, wishing I knew how to make things right. Charlie would know. In

New York City, he said sweet things to girls that made them smile and go all soft-eyed. Even though I pulled my share, I lacked his finesse.

I look up and Charlie is sitting beside Harper on the bench, his arms hooked around the back and his body so close to hers, I wonder why she doesn't feel it, doesn't *see* him.

"We fucked up good, didn't we, Solo?" he says.

I just stare at him as he reaches across the table and—just as if we were back at infantry school—snatches a strip of bacon from my plate. It doesn't levitate in midair, and beside Charlie, Harper crunches a bite of toast, unaware that there are three of us at this table.

"I mean . . ." Charlie folds the whole strip of bacon into his mouth and chews for a moment. "I'm dead and you're seeing things that aren't really there, and we have no one else to blame."

"We should have told somebody about the kid," I say, and Harper looks at me.

"What?" she asks.

Charlie turns his head to look at her and I see the gash in the side of his neck, the skin torn open, and dark dried blood crusted around the edges.

My stomach churns and the fork clatters as it hits the plate. I bolt for the restroom, barely making it to the stall before I puke up eggs and bacon. My eyes burning and nose dripping, I stand in the stall—holding on to the walls to keep from falling over—until the heaving stops. My mouth tastes sour and my heart is beating too fast.

"Travis, are you okay?" Harper pokes her head into the men's room as I'm splashing cold water on my face. For a split second I hate her for seeing me this way, but it's not her fault my brain is playing tricks on me. No, I'm not okay. I'm losing my fucking mind.

"I need to go."

"Yeah, sure." She looks confused and I can't blame her. First I hit on her in a dive bar. Then I showed up outside her house in the middle of the night. Now I'm in the men's room of the Waffle House, where I just flushed away my breakfast. "I'll, um . . ." She looks at my reflection in the mirror and I can't tell what she's thinking. "I'll take care of the bill."

"I've got it," I say, but the door thumps closed behind her. I pat my pocket, but it's empty. Just as well she didn't hear me. I forgot my wallet, too.

We don't talk on the drive to my house. At least not until she pulls the Land Rover into the driveway.

"Feeling better now?" Harper asks.

I can't tell her I saw Charlie, that back there in the restaurant he *talked* to me. Because what Marine—what person, really—wants to admit his brain is scrambled? What girl is going to want to date *that* guy? "I guess. Thanks."

Despite my weirdness, though, something has changed between us. Like she got out of her system what has been festering since middle school. I don't think she hates me anymore. Or else she thinks I'm pathetic and feels sorry for me, which is not ideal, but still an improvement over hating me. "Hey, Harper, can I ask you something?"

"Okay." Her expression is guarded. Wary.

"You could have brought me straight home, but you didn't," I say. "Why?"

She doesn't look at me, just stares straight ahead through the front windshield. "I have to go. I'm going to be late for work."

I don't press the question as I get out of the Rover. Her non-answer is enough for now. "I'll see you later, Harper."

* * *

My mom is alone at the kitchen island when I go inside, her hands curled around a cup of coffee. She gives me a tired smile, then glances at the clock. "Have you been out all this time?"

"Sort of."

Used to be she'd try to ground me for staying out all night. Now she doesn't even ask where I've been. Her eyes are ringed with sadness. "Coffee?"

I'm so tired I can barely see straight, but I guess I can stay up a few minutes longer with my mom. I scrub my hand over my face. I need a shave. "Sure, thanks."

She reaches up to the open cupboard and I notice she's not wearing her rings. They're lying in the soap dish at the edge of the sink, which is odd. She takes them off when she washes the dishes, but she always puts them right back on. She fills a USMC Mom mug with coffee and slides it to me.

"You okay?" I ask.

She nods with her head down, so I can't see her face, but when she looks up there are tears in her eyes. Shit. This night is never going to end. She wipes her nose with a tissue. "Your dad didn't come home last night."

"What the—? Why? Where is he?"

"I don't know," she says. "I called his cell, but he didn't answer."

Something is not right here. "Mom, what's going on?"

"He—we haven't been getting along very well this past year. And, I don't know, maybe it's my own fault."

I move to her side of the island and put my arms around her. It's hard to be affectionate with her—and not only because I've been away so long. I'm not used to this. She collapses against my chest, her words and sobs spilling out together in a flood.

"While you were in Afghanistan, I went a little—well, I went a little crazy," she says. "You have no idea how afraid I was for you. I was on the Internet until all hours of the night, talking to other Marine parents and googling your name to make sure you were still alive. Whenever I saw a news article that said US troops had been killed, I was terrified the doorbell would ring and someone would tell me you were dead. Then they'd release the names and I'd cry with relief that it wasn't my son and then cry more because it was someone else's son. I was obsessive about keeping my cell phone charged and I checked it a million times a day so I wouldn't miss your call."

Mom wipes her eyes, but she can't stop the flow of tears. "I was so worried about you that I didn't pay attention when your dad started staying later at the dealerships. At least, that's where I thought he was."

This is not her fault. It's mine.

"He's having an affair," she says.

We're all assholes. Me. Ryan. Dad. All for the same damn reason, even if what motivates us is different. Me being here, comforting her, isn't absolution.

"I'm going to kill him."

Mom sucks in a snotty breath and pulls back. "No. It's okay. I didn't mean—" She smoothes her hand over the damp spot on my shirt. "I didn't mean to put this on your shoulders. God knows you've got enough on your plate." She looks up at me. "Travis, have you been fighting?"

"Not exactly. Long story," I say. "Have you slept?"

She shakes her head and gestures toward a to-do list lying on the island. Grocery shopping. Cookies for the cheerleader car wash/bake sale. Dry cleaner. I crush the list. "Sleep first. And Dad can pick up his own dry cleaning."

Mom's eyes go watery again. "You're such a good man, Travis."

If she knew the pain I wanted to inflict on my own

father, she'd know I'm not even close to being a good man.

"Go get some sleep, Mom."

I finally reach my own room and collapse on the bed—too tired to think about Dad or Harper or even that the mattress is too soft. If I have any nightmares, they're gone before I wake up again.

Chapter 4

There's a ceiling fan revolving slowly overhead and I wonder why I smell oatmeal cookies. Then it hits me again that I'm still in Florida, and I wonder if the remembering will ever become second nature. I glance at the clock. I've only had a couple hours of sleep, but I'm wide-awake.

I swap my skivvies for a pair of swim trunks and go out to the pool. Most of us lost weight in-country. Because even though MREs are high in calories and designed to sustain a person through the day on just one or two, they can't replace what you lose hiking around in 110-degree heat with eighty pounds of gear on your back. I was almost always hungry. But just because I can stand to gain a few pounds doesn't mean I want to get lazy and fat on leave.

I'm about five laps in when I see a shadow at the edge of

the pool. I surface and find my dad standing there wearing a pale blue golf shirt and matching plaid Bermuda shorts.

"Hey, champ." He sounds like a tool. Champ is an old nickname from when I was still drinking the Dean Stephenson Kool-Aid. He alternated it with sport, tiger, and killer. I guess the latter is the most accurate now, but they all come off as used-car-salesman phony. We're not buddies because he's deemed me worthy again.

I hang on the edge of the pool and wait for him to say whatever it is he wants to say, my eyes pinned to his. His Adam's apple drops as he swallows nervously and I feel a surge of satisfaction. For so long I was afraid of him, but now I'm bigger and stronger. "What do you say we go hit the gun range?" he says. "Get out of your mom's hair so she can get ready for tonight's dinner."

"What dinner?"

"We're having Don and Becky Michalski over."

My friend Derek's dad, Don, is the guy who coaches loudly from the stands and gets mad when the players, coaches, and referees don't do what he says. He gets in fights with other parents. He's been banned for life from Ida Baker High School after punching their soccer coach. My mom hates him, and his wife is embarrassed to be seen with him in public, so I don't know why Mom would agree to cook for him. Unless . . . it's not about Don. It's about Becky.

"I think I'll hang out here," I say. "Give Mom a hand."

"You sure?" Confusion flickers across his face. "I'd like to see you in action."

I've never voluntarily hung out with my mother, but right now it beats this lame attempt to show me he's a cool dad. Also, I scored top marks in boot camp for marksmanship. It's probably for the best if he doesn't see me in action.

"I'm positive."

He stands there as I swim away, and I can see his shadow on the water for a while, as if he's waiting for me to change my mind. It takes everything in me not to pull myself out of the pool and beat the shit out of him. Instead, I swim.

I'm a hypocrite after what happened last night with Paige, but me hooking up with my ex-girlfriend behind my brother's back is not the same as my dad cheating on his wife. Paige and I have used each other this way for years, stretching away from each other and snapping back like a rubber band. The only person who stands to get hurt is Ryan, but it's not as if he's going to marry Paige Manning, either.

Down in the kitchen, Mom is her pulled-together self again, except for the tiredness lurking at the corners of her eyes. Her purse is looped over her arm, the crumpled list in one hand and the keys to a brand-new Suburban—one of the perks of being married to the owner of a car dealership—in the other. "Want to ride along?"

"Sure."

She looks surprised. "Really?"

"Really." I jam my foot into one of my tan combat boots. On the outside it's scuffed and worn from continuous wear, a spatter of rusty bloodstains across the toe. Inside it smells like shit, but I don't have any other shoes except my running shoes, and I hate those. I bought a pair of Sambas when I graduated boot camp but didn't lock them up at infantry school and someone stole them. "So what was Dad's excuse?"

"He says Steve Fischer invited him over for a drink. He didn't want to drink and drive, so he spent the night," she says. "He called to tell me he was okay before he went to play golf."

I follow her to the garage. "You know I'm going to kill him, right?"

A ghost of a smile plays across her lips as she starts the Suburban, as if she can imagine it and she likes the idea. Then her face rearranges into something more Mom-appropriate and slightly disapproving. "Travis, he's your father."

He doesn't get a free pass because we share DNA. If anything, that's even more reason to kick his ass. "You can't let him get away with it, Mom," I say. "Just because—"

"Let's talk about something else." Her hands grip the steering wheel with such ferocity that she could probably rip it right out of the dashboard. Subject closed. I guess that's only fair. She's been artful at avoiding the subject of Afghanistan, and I suspect it's because she read an article somewhere on the Internet that said I'll talk about it when

I'm ready. I'm not sure I'll ever be ready, but I guess I owe her the same respect.

"None of my clothes fit and I need new shoes," I say.

Her smile shifts to wide. "Now, that I can do."

On San Carlos, we pass a veterans' club. It's a sketchy little place not affiliated with any other club in the country, but there are always cars in the lot. Pops, who was a Marine with the 3/7 in Korea, brought me there once for lunch when he was down from Green Bay for a visit. "Hey, um— do you want to get some lunch?"

I'm not really the type to join a veterans' organization— especially since I'm still active duty—but I could use a beer and . . . I don't know. Maybe I won't feel so out of place there.

"Here?" Mom eyes the place skeptically. "Um—sure."

Inside, the veterans' club is more of a dump than I remember. The walls are painted with emblems from all the armed forces branches, only they're amateurish and out of proportion. The tables wobble and the chairs don't match, but the bartender gives me a membership application he calls a formality.

"Iraq?" he asks.

"Afghanistan."

"Marine?"

"Yes, sir."

"Semper Fi, son." He shakes my hand and I see his *Death Before Dishonor* tattoo. Kevlar got one exactly like it on his back after he graduated boot camp, and the saltier Marines in our platoon ragged on him mercilessly about it. "You're welcome to stay for lunch," the bartender says. "The special today is fish sandwiches with fries and coleslaw."

I order two sandwiches and a pitcher of beer, which he draws for me without so much as blinking.

"Travis." Mom frowns as I pour the beer into plastic cups. She leans forward, keeping her voice low. As if we're doing something naughty. "You're not twenty-one."

"I am a veteran of a foreign war." I hand her a cup. "More importantly, I'm thirsty."

At first we don't talk about Dad. We don't talk about anything, really. We drink beer, agree the fish sandwiches taste good, and speculate on what kind of fish it is.

"I've been thinking about seeing a lawyer." Mom refills our glasses. I wipe my mouth with the back of my hand and she hands me a paper napkin. Dining room manners tend to lapse when there's no dining room—or even a table. Most of the time we ate sitting on the ground, where there was no lack of places to sit, and "Hey, save me a seat" was a running joke between me and Charlie.

"Yeah?" I ask.

She nods. "I'm—I'm kind of scared."

"Why?"

"We've been together a long time," she says. "I don't know how to be alone. Or what I would do with myself."

"You could go back to school."

She gives me a wobbly smile. "Maybe you and I both could."

I have three years of active duty left, but she thinks I'll use my GI Bill to get an education. I don't tell her I still have no interest in college. I can't envision myself as a teacher or an accountant or a lawyer. Or even married with kids.

Charlie always knew what he wanted. Some nights in-country, we'd lie on our backs on the ground with our boots propped up against the schoolhouse wall, pass a cigarette back and forth, and he'd talk about how he wanted to go to culinary school when he got out of the Marines.

"I want to be a chef, Solo," he said. "But not like those pretentious guys who make teeny-tiny dishes no one can pronounce, you know? I want to have a restaurant where regular people can try gourmet food without feeling stupid or wondering which fork to use."

I never pointed out that most regular people aren't all that interested in trying food like that, because it was his dream and who was I to stomp all over it?

"What about you, Trav?" he asked.

"I don't know, dude," I said. "Maybe I'll go recon."

He laughed because we learned real fast that you always make fun of the hard chargers who talk about reenlisting or going recon. Reconnaissance Marines are specially trained scouts. Elite. A lot of guys join the Marines wanting to go recon because they think it's cool, but they go through some seriously rigorous training. I was only a year out of high school and no closer to knowing what I wanted to do with my future. I was only joking with Charlie but now—I don't know. I think I could do it.

Now Charlie is dead, and I'm having trouble even picturing a future with me in it. Still, I humor my mom. "Maybe. Anyway, you should see a lawyer. I'll go with you if you want."

Her smile slides off her face and I can tell the beer buzz has dredged up some doubt. She glances at her watch. "Travis." She hiccups. "We need to go. We haven't bought groceries yet."

"Give me the keys." I settle the tab, turn in my membership application, and follow my mom out to the Suburban. She keeps missing the slot on her seat belt, so I have to do it for her. "We should go home," I say. "We can shop later."

"Your dad will be mad." She yawns. "I want a nap."

I laugh. I've never seen her this way. "Okay, then, a nap it is."

Dad is watching golf on TV, a bottle of beer in his hand, when we get home.

"Oh, good, you're here," he says. "Linda, did you remember to buy beer?"

She nods and holds up three fingers, then uses her other hand to bend one finger down so she's only holding up two. "Two pitchers."

My mom is wasted. It's kind of . . . cool.

His eyes narrow. "Have you been drinking?" He turns

his glare on me. Cool Dad is gone. Real Dad is back. "Travis, you got your mother drunk?"

I shrug. "You can blame me if you want."

"Why didn't you stop her?" He's on his feet now, eyes blazing, voice sliding up an octave. "We've got company coming tonight and nothing is ready." He turns back to her. "I don't know why I'm surprised. You have all the time in the world to buy socks for Travis and to google all night with strangers about your son in Afghanistan, but I ask you for one little thing—"

"This isn't about Travis," she says.

"Of course it's about *Travis*," he spits. "It's *always* about Travis."

"Mom." I keep my eyes on him. "Why don't you go up and take that nap? I'll take care of everything."

"But—"

"It's okay," I say. "I've got it under control."

She plants a sloppy kiss on my cheek. "You're such a good boy."

I am nowhere near good right now.

"I thought the military would have matured you," Dad says when she's out of earshot. "But you're the same disrespectful little punk you were before you left."

I grab the front of his shirt in my fist. It takes this little punk no effort at all to pull him toward me. He looks scared, and he should, because there's not much in this world more frightening than a pissed-off grunt. "You know what I was doing at six o'clock this morning? Sitting in the kitchen with Mom, who waited all night for you to come home. So don't fucking talk to *me* about *respect*."

He doesn't say anything and his eyes are wide. I shouldn't feel good about that, but I do.

"You want to be pathetic and screw around behind Mom's back because she pays attention to someone other than you, that's your business," I say. "But I won't be your excuse."

I shove him a little as I let go and he staggers backward. If I wanted to drop him, he'd be on the floor right now, but this was my warning shot.

"I'm going to the grocery store." I grab the keys to the Suburban. "Gotta make sure *Becky* feels welcome."

Dad's tanned face goes pale. He pulls out his wallet. "Do you—do you need some cash?"

"Not from you."

It isn't until I get to the Winn-Dixie that I realize I have a problem—I didn't bring Mom's list. I have no clue what people cook for dinner parties, even for people they hate.

I head for the meat department.

"Can I help you?" the butcher asks.

"What would you cook if you were having a, um— dinner party?"

Jesus, I feel like an idiot.

"Well, a roast is always tasty," he offers. "Or pork chops. Or even lamb chops."

Lamb chops? I walk away from the counter and stand

in front of the cooler full of meat. I have no idea what to buy. I don't even know what most of it is. This is a nightmare.

"Do you need help?" a female voice from behind asks.

I'm about to throw an offended no over my shoulder when Harper comes up alongside me, all green eyes and tousled hair. I could probably look at her forever and not get tired of that face. "If I say yes will you think less of me?"

She shrugs, but I can see a smile at the corner of her mouth. "I already do think less of you."

"You're not planning to hit me again, are you?"

"Well, I wasn't *planning* on it, but I try to keep my options open." She puts her plastic shopping basket in my cart. "So you're having a dinner party?"

"Yes, I mean, no. My mom is, but she's—not feeling well, so I figured I'd come buy the stuff, take it home, and cook it."

She cocks her head, skeptical. "Do you know how to cook, Travis?"

"How hard can it be?" Her eyebrows lift and she doesn't say anything at all, which makes me laugh. "Okay, no. But I want to do something nice for her."

Harper's smile is like standing in a patch of sunshine and feels like a reward. "So maybe you should try something a little less complicated, but still good," she says. "Like . . . okay, I have an idea."

As I follow her to the produce section, I notice her jeans

are faded to white in spots with a circle worn into the fabric of the right back pocket where someone once kept a can of dip. Thrift store jeans. I used to buy most of my clothes from thrift stores, too. I liked that they were already broken-in and soft from wear.

On the way, she gives me a tutorial on choosing the freshest tomatoes, but I'm not really listening. I'm thinking about Becky Michalski. Why would my dad have an affair with her? She's unremarkable, especially compared to Mom. Seems to me, she's the ultimate loser in this scenario. Going from Don to my dad is kind of a lateral move.

"Travis, are you in there?" Harper is waving her hand in front of my face.

"I nearly punched my dad today." I'm not sure what possesses me to blurt this to Harper Gray in the middle of the produce section of the Winn-Dixie, but there's something I trust about her.

"Why?"

"He's cheating on my mom."

"I . . . wow, I'm sorry." She looks up at me and what I see in her eyes isn't pity or even satisfaction that karma is coming back to bite me for the way I treated her in middle school. She just looks sad. "Want to talk about it?"

"Not really."

Those are the words that come out of my mouth, but then I find myself leaning against the vegetable bin, telling her everything. Including the part about getting my mom drunk.

Harper smiles at that. "That's sweet . . . in a weird sort of way."

She moves so we're both blocking the avocados, her arm brushing against mine. It makes the hair on the back of my neck prickle. "My mom left when I was ten," she says. "She went back to Denmark to take care of my grandma, who was dying of cancer, and never came back."

"Oh, shit. I had no idea."

"It was a long time ago." Her shoulders lift in a careless little bounce that seems to have more care in it than she lets on. "For a long time I thought it was my fault. Like, if I had been better, she wouldn't have left. Then I realized it had nothing to do with me and I wanted to punch her. Only she wasn't here."

An old guy comes up and we have to move out of his way. Harper leads me to a bin filled with rubber-banded clumps of herbs. They all look the same—green and bushy—but she explains we're looking for basil.

"Have you had any contact with your mom since she left?" I ask, handing her a bundle of basil.

"She sends me birthday cards every year," she says as I follow her to the pasta aisle. "Only she puts Danish kroner in the card instead of American dollars. It's not even worth getting converted." Harper drops a couple of boxes of penne pasta in the cart. "For graduation, she sent me a ticket to Copenhagen."

"Did you go?"

"Yeah . . . she, um, lives in this communal house in Christiania with a bunch of other people, so the entire time I was there she was either painting in her studio or getting stoned with her twenty-two-year-old boyfriend. I slept on a couch that smelled like cat pee."

"That sucks."

She nods as she grabs a can of black olives from the shelf. "Copenhagen was cool, though. I went to LEGOLAND by myself and got this cute keychain."

Harper dangles her keys from the end of her finger. The keychain is a little yellow LEGO duck.

"Did you punch her?"

"No." Her nose crinkles when she smiles. "But I don't miss her anymore." We stop at the seafood counter. "You order a couple of pounds of shrimp. I'll get the bread and cheese and then we'll be done."

Right now, if Harper asked me to swim out into the Gulf of Mexico and catch the shrimp with my bare hands, I'd do it. By the time the guy behind the seafood counter is finished wrapping the shrimp, she's back with a long loaf of bread and a block of hard white cheese that's definitely not the processed orange goo I've been eating. I still have no idea what I'll be cooking, but it looks impressive. Too good for the Michalskis. Too good for my dad.

"So it's just been you and your dad?" I ask, trying to imagine what it would have been like growing up with only Mom. "I'm surprised he never got remarried."

"He's never really dated that much," Harper says. "But now . . . I don't know. He spends a lot of time e-mailing back and forth with some woman he knew before he met my mom, which—it makes me feel weird."

She pushes the cart into the checkout lane, and when the cashier is done ringing it all up—including the stuff in her basket—I pay the bill. "So what do I do with all this stuff?"

"I'll write it down for you."

"You could come over and—"

"I think you can manage." Our eyes meet for a moment and I look for something. Anything. But then her gaze falls to her flip-flops with a shyness that kills me in the best possible way. She reaches out and gives me a playful punch in the arm. "Adapt and overcome, Marine."

I laugh. I want to say more, but she starts getting that deer-in-the-headlights look, as if she might bolt any second. I unlock the Suburban and take out the notepad my mom has kept in the center console of every car she's ever had. Our fingers touch as I hand it to Harper, and her cheeks go pink. Interesting. Frustrating, but interesting.

"It's really simple," she says, writing something on the pad. "Roast the tomatoes, sauté the shrimp, boil the pasta, toss the ingredients together, then grate some cheese over the top. Serve the bread on the side."

"Sounds foolproof."

"Yeah, well . . ." She hands me the notepad. "You're cooking it."

We stand there in the parking lot, just looking at each other. The afternoon sun brings out slivers of gold and red in her hair and the freckles on her nose—and again I have the urge to kiss her. Instead, I reach out and give her hair a gentle tug. "Thanks. I couldn't have done it without you."

"No problem." She waves me off in a little it-was-nothing-gesture, but I'm pretty sure it was something. I'm just not sure what.

* * *

I hear music pumping from the house before I'm even out of the car. At first I think it's Ryan, but it's not the ridiculous pop metal crap he likes. It's Aretha Franklin wailing about R-E-S-P-E-C-T.

Uh-oh.

I open the door and my mom is sitting at her favorite spot at the kitchen island with a glass of white wine at her elbow. Her eyes are red and swollen.

"Are you okay?" I ask as I place the grocery bags on the counter. "What happened?"

Mom turns down the stereo and rubs her nose on the sleeve of a ratty old football T-shirt that used to be mine. She only wears cast-off shirts when she's cleaning house. "I told him to leave."

"What?"

"Your dad," she says. "When I woke up, we had the same fight we've been having for the past year about what a terrible, neglectful person I am because I've been worried sick about you. So I canceled on the Michalskis and told him to stay wherever he stayed last night until he hears from my attorney."

"Damn, Mom. Way to grow a pair."

A hiccup-giggle escapes her, then her eyes fill with fresh tears. Oh, shit. Not more crying. "Did I do the right thing, Travis?"

It would be easy to lie and say yes. I don't care if Dad stays or goes, but she loves him.

"I don't know."

"Maybe this is all my fault." She reaches for her cell phone. "Maybe I could call—"

"No." I cover her hand with mine. "He needs to decide what's important."

"You're right. It's just that—he's still my husband."

"I know."

Mom sniffles. "You bought groceries?"

"Yeah, so, you know, turn up your music or whatever," I say. "I've got it under control."

Her eyebrows lift over the rim of her wineglass, but she doesn't protest. She cranks the volume on Aretha. Not as loud as it was before, but still loud enough that we don't have to talk. Which is good, because I don't know what I could possibly say to make her feel better.

"Do you need some help?" she asks.

"I can do it."

The corners of her mouth pull up in a tiny smile. "You've always been this way."

"Like what?"

"Independent," she says. "Stubborn. As soon as you could talk, your answer for everything was 'Me do it' and you'd get angry if I tried to help you. Even then you were trying to get away from me."

She takes a sip of wine. "I only took the job at your school so I could have a little part of your life. I always envied that your dad got to spend so much time with you."

"Really?"

"I give you credit for sticking with football as long as you did," Mom says. "Especially when you hated it."

"Well, just so you know," I say, pulling the tomatoes from the plastic bag, holding all three of them in one hand. "I was never trying to get away from *you*."

"You have no idea how happy that makes me." Except she starts sniffling like she's going to cry, and I don't want that again.

"Hey, Mom?"

"Yeah, Trav?"

"How do you roast tomatoes?"

She smiles. "Would you like some help?"

I nod. "Yeah, I would."

Chapter 5

It's a quarter to five and I'm still awake.

I dress in the dark, then take the keys to the Suburban from the hook next to the garage door and drive with no destination in mind. US 41 is empty this time of night, but I enjoy it. My mom always assumed I was up to no good when I stayed out all night, but most of the time I was just driving around. I think about turning the SUV north and heading to North Carolina, but I don't have my stuff and I'm not really allowed to go back yet.

We were back from Afghanistan a couple of days when Sergeant Peralta—my squad leader—called me aside.

"Just wanted to check in," he said. "You doing okay?"

"Yeah, I'm good."

"You sure?" he asked. "Because you seem like you're dragging ass. That's not like you."

The nightmares were keeping me up most nights. "Just tired, I guess."

"Listen, I'm concerned that you're not dealing with Charlie's death," he said. "As a friend, I'm telling you that you need to get your shit together before anyone higher up the chain notices."

"I'm fine," I said. "I just need to go buy a brand-new Mustang and shack up with a stripper."

Peralta laughed, because we'd just finished sitting through a two-hour stand-down on money management—basically, that we shouldn't throw it away on expensive cars, blow it at the casino, or marry girls who would spend it all and dump us for another Marine. Thing is, I wasn't sure what he was saying. Did he want me to see a shrink? And what would happen to me—to my career—if I did?

"You're a good Marine, Travis, and I want to see you succeed," he said. "So I strongly suggest you take two extra weeks beyond the two-week post-deployment leave to work things out."

"Are you making this suggestion as a friend, too?"

"I'll leave that up to you to decide," he said.

I didn't want to use that much of my leave—and I sure as hell didn't want to come home—but it was an order wrapped in a suggestion. And I respected Peralta too much to disobey.

* * *

I pull into the parking lot at the Waffle House, one of the few all-night places in town. I go inside and Harper is standing behind the counter, wearing a gray uniform shirt and black apron. Her hair is scraped up in a knot. When she sees me, her eyebrows pull together for a second before her lips stretch into a fake smile. "Hi, welcome to Waffle House."

"You work here?" I sit on one of the stools. There's a button pinned to her apron that says *If I had half a mind I'd still be twice as smart as you.*

She rolls her eyes. "No, idiot, I just wear the shirt so I can get free food." I laugh as she reaches across the counter and plinks my forehead. It's a playful gesture. A welcome change from punching me in the face. "Are you stalking me, Travis?"

"What? No!"

Her eyebrows lift as she crosses her arms over her chest—as if she doesn't believe me—but she doesn't look mad. "You've shown up where I've been four times in the last three days."

"Completely coincidental," I say as she puts a coffee cup on the counter and fills it from a full pot. "Except, you know, for the time I showed up at your house, but that was more like . . . unintentionally intentional. The question is, do you mind?"

She ignores me. "Are you going to order?"

"Let's try the All-Star again."

"Over easy with bacon?"

I grin. "Aw, you remembered."

She flips me off, calls my order to the grill cook, and turns back to me. "What are you doing tonight?"

"Eating at Waffle House?"

"No, I mean *tonight* tonight," she says. "After you go to sleep and wake back up again."

Not really sure where she's going with this, since I'll probably stay awake, but whatever it is, I'm game. "Anything you want."

"Anything?" The way she smiles makes me wonder what I've just agreed to do. "Perfect. I'll pick you up at nine p.m."

* * *

"So what are we doing?" I ask, glancing into the backseat of the Land Rover. Lying across the seat is a small shovel, along with a black plastic tarp and a flashlight with a piece of red film covering the lens. "Burying a body?"

Harper throws a devious smile in my direction. "Maybe."

So fucking cool.

"We're nest-sitting." She hands me a large foam cup of coffee.

"What does that mean?"

"Well, we're in the middle of sea turtle hatching season," she explains. "It's been fifty-five days since this one particular nest was laid, so tonight should be the night."

I'm not an especially romantic person, but when a beautiful girl invites a guy to the beach at night, sea turtles are not usually involved. Also, this is not something I'd have expected from Harper. "So we're . . . helping?"

"In a sense. We give them as many advantages as we can without disturbing the natural process," she says. "I brought you because I figured you'd be good at digging."

Marines carry small folding shovels called entrenching tools. E-tools, for short. We use them to dig holes for sleeping, burning trash, fighting, and taking a dump. So, yes, I am very good at digging. "That the only reason?"

She gives me a tiny bit-lip smile that knocks the wind out of my chest. "Maybe."

On the way to the beach, Harper explains that I'll dig a trench from the nest to the water while she sets up the tarp. It's attached at intervals to wooden stakes so it can be positioned around the nest and along the trench. A funnel to keep the baby sea turtles pointed in the right direction and keep away raccoons, crabs, and anything else that might want to eat them.

"So how long have you been turtle-sitting?"

"A couple of years," she says. "I'm planning to study marine biology."

It's tempting to make a joke about Marines and biology, but her smile says this is important to her, and I don't want to ruin it with a stupid joke. "That's very cool."

"What about you?" Harper presses a button on the CD player and Joe Strummer sings about redemption. "Do you think you'll go to college when you're done with the Marines?"

"I don't know," I say. "I've still got a lot of time left, so I've been thinking about doing the basic recon course." Not sure why I'm telling her this, but it's as if I can't help myself. I swear, if anyone wants to torture secrets out of me, apparently all they have to do is put me in a room with her. I only joked about recon with Charlie, but now that I've told someone else, it feels even more like a real option.

"What does that mean?" she asks.

"Reconnaissance Marines are kind of like special forces," I say. "Sort of like how the Navy has SEALs or the Army has Rangers."

"So basically you want to do something even more dangerous than you're already doing?"

I laugh. "I guess."

"You like the Marines, don't you?"

"I don't know." I shrug. "Except for the part where people shoot at you, it's not all that different from any other job. There are things I like and things that suck," I say. "So where are you going to school?"

"The College of the Atlantic. It's up in Maine." She parks the Rover in a spot in the deserted beach lot and cuts the engine.

"That's pretty far from home." I open my door. Pretty far from anywhere I'll be, too, which kind of sucks.

"Not as far as Afghanistan," she says.

"Good point."

Harper gets out of the car as I start taking the supplies from the backseat. She opens the door opposite me. "COA has a really good marine science program. One of the best, really."

"I had no idea you were so smart," I say, stepping out onto the sand. "Or that you still played with Barbies when you were thirteen."

She laughs and punches me on the arm. "There's a *lot* you don't know about me."

"I guess," I say. "But I, um—I'd like to."

She goes quiet as she kicks off her flip-flops, and she reminds me of a turtle, sticking her head out to investigate, then pulling back at the first sign of danger. I want to tell her I won't hurt her, but what proof does she have of that? Thing is, I don't want to hurt her. Harper brings out something different in me than Paige. Something better. At least, I want to believe that.

"So . . ." I change the subject. "The eggs?"

"It could take all night for them to hatch." Harper moves

past me and I fight the urge to grab her arm and stop her, momentarily forgetting there are no bombs buried here. In Afghanistan, they could be anywhere. One time we were sweeping a road because we knew there was a bomb on it, but even with a metal detector we couldn't find it. We gave up, got in the truck, drove a little farther down the road, and hit the bomb we'd been looking for. None of us were hurt— just a little tossed around—but it messed up the truck. Even after my brain gets the memo that we are not going to blow up on Bonita Beach, I can't stop my eyes from scanning the sand for explosives.

"Is this a problem?" she asks.

For a moment I have to remember what we were talking about, but then I look up at her, the sea breeze lifting the stray hairs around her face. "Nope, not a problem at all."

The nest is on a dark portion of the beach, not far from a three-level house with a caged pool. The house is still shuttered for the off season. It's quiet. Only the soft *whoosh* of the waves and the round white moon, scattering its reflection across the water. If I've missed anything about home, it's this.

Harper leads me to a miniature crime scene. The nest looks like the remnants of a washed-out sandcastle, marked by a crisscrossing of yellow caution tape and a warning sign to stay away.

"The tarp goes here." She points the red flashlight beam at a spot above the nest, then sweeps it to the water side of the nest. "And the trench starts here. All the way down to the water."

"How deep?"

"About ankle." Harper starts unrolling the tarp. "It has to be deep enough to keep them from climbing out and heading for an artificial light source."

I start digging. The sand here is more dense than in Afghanistan, where it's the consistency of powder. It came out with my snot when I blew my nose, from my ears when I swabbed them, and the first spit when brushing my teeth was always brown. At one of our outposts there was a well, and sometimes we washed in the irrigation canals, but we never were truly clean.

I'm halfway to the water when I hear a splintering crack.

* * *

I'm crossing a shallow canal between fields with Charlie and an Afghan soldier behind me, when a round from an AK-47 zings past me like an angry bee.

I slide into the canal at once, the muddy water filling my boots and creeping up the legs of my trousers. Charlie is standing still on the edge of the canal, an unmoving target.

"Charlie, get down!" I try to scramble up the bank to grab him, but slip as the mud crumbles beneath my boot, my hand clutching at his ankle. "Get your ass down!"

He slides down the canal bank as a shot cracks over his head. The Afghan soldier on my other side fires his automatic weapon, spraying blindly at where he thinks the Taliban are hiding. I peer over the edge of the bank, trying to figure out where the fire is coming from.

Crack!

* * *

"Travis!" Harper's voice cuts through the memory and, just like that, it's over. Except I'm lying on the sand and she's standing over me with a broken stake—the source of the splintering sound—in her hand. My heart is racing so fast I'm afraid it's going to explode, and I can't catch my breath. "Are you okay?" she asks.

"No." I didn't mean to say that. "I mean . . ." I'm so embarrassed, I can't even look at her. Also, the wetness of the sand has penetrated the front of my shorts, and my nuts are cold. "I'm fine."

That firefight happened on our very first patrol and it happened so fast that I don't know if Charlie froze out of fear or if he thought he was invincible. And even now I don't remember if he fired his weapon. All I know was that he was lucky that day.

Harper sits down beside me and reaches for my hand. Her fingers graze calluses, ruptured blisters, and scars from cuts that took too long to heal because my hands were always dirty. She doesn't say anything. She just squeezes.

"You should probably stay away from me," I say, resting my head on my knees. "I'm a mess."

"That was really scary," Harper says. "You were yelling and I had no idea what to do. I can't even imagine what it must be like for you."

"It fucking sucks." I grab the shovel and fling it away as hard and as far as I can. "I just want to be normal again."

But what has been done can't be undone. My best friend is dead and I'm never going to be the same Travis Stephenson.

Harper doesn't look at me as she pushes to her feet and walks over to get the shovel. I'm filled with white-hot rage at her for being so kind, but it burns itself out by the time she comes back. "Maybe," she says, holding out the shovel, "it's time to find a new normal."

"I, um—I'm sorry."

She smiles at me. "Don't apologize, Travis, just dig."

Half an hour later, I collapse on a sheet Harper spread beside the nest. My T-shirt is sticking to my skin, so I pull it over my head before I lie back. Stars freckle the sky, and the sand beneath the sheet is cool against my warm skin. That was the one really amazing thing about Afghanistan. There are no city lights to clog the night sky, so it feels like you're seeing the whole universe. I close my eyes.

"Nice trench." Harper drops beside me on the sheet and hugs her knees to her chest. "You did a good job."

"So now what?"

"We wait."

Harper shivers a little. August in Fort Myers is usually

sweltering, even at night, but there's a front moving in and the sea breeze has kicked up a little. I hand her the sweatshirt I brought. "Do you think they'll hatch tonight?"

"There are signs," she says. "The nest has collapsed a little in spots. Just small shifts in the sand that suggest movement. We might only get one or two tonight, or we might get all of them." She gives me the type of smile that makes me care about sea turtles. "It's exciting, isn't it?"

Perversely, yes.

"I can think of worse ways to spend the night."

She pulls on my sweatshirt. "Like what?"

"Every single night in Afghanistan," I say, but it's not really true. We had some good times. I tell her about the time Charlie's mom sent us pizza—canned sauce, premade crust, pepperoni, mushrooms. She even included a metal pizza pan and one of those rolling cutter tools.

"We dug a fire pit, put a grate over it, and barbecued it," I say. "It was kind of burned on the bottom and the freeze-dried mozzarella wasn't fully melted on top, but it tasted so good. Like home."

"Charlie is one of your buddies?"

"He was."

Her smile fades. "I'm sorry, Travis. I didn't know."

"I know."

"I heard Ryan talking at school once," she says. "He said he wasn't sure about the details, but that you were a hero. That you saved some people's lives or something."

"Ryan doesn't know anything." I sit up and tug my T-shirt back on. I hate my brother right now for using my life as some sort of . . . bragging right. Especially when there really isn't anything to brag about. "I really don't mean to be rude, but I'd rather not talk about this."

"I'm sorry."

"No, Harper, you didn't do anything wrong. It's just— I'm not a hero," I say. "If I were . . ." Charlie might still be alive. "I'm just not."

She doesn't say anything right away, then she shoulder-bumps me. "You *do* have superior digging skills."

I laugh. "Yeah, well, this one time at boot camp they gave me a medal for shoveling. You need a hole dug, I'm your man."

I sneak a look at her while she's laughing. My sweatshirt is huge on her, but it looks so good. As if she belongs in that sweatshirt. And I don't even want to think about what that means. Instead, I think about leaning toward her, kissing her. Except I think too long and she's on her feet, her eyes wide as if she can read my mind.

"We should—" Harper swings her head toward the nest. "The turtles."

I can't figure her out at all. She doesn't behave the way most girls I've met behave. An awkward vibe zigzags between us as I follow her to the nest. She shines the red-covered flashlight and makes an excited little squeak. In the muted red glow, a tiny head and a pair of flippers wiggle their way out of the sand. Harper reaches for my hand and squeezes my fingers, telegraphing her happiness through me. I don't do anything.

A second head pops through the sand as the first baby turtle flips his way to the mouth of the trench. This is only the beginning. I have to admit—I want to pick up the little bastard and carry him.

"What happens when they reach the water?" I ask. "There's a whole new set of predators there we can't do anything about."

Harper laughs. "It almost sounds like you care."

"Do you think I'd be sitting out here on a beach in the middle of the night if I didn't?"

She lets go of my hand, her expression impossible to read, and unzips her backpack. The sound is magnified by her silence. She takes out a clipboard. "I need to keep notes."

The first little turtle is flipping his way down the trench and I can't help but like the little dude. Or girl. I wonder how you tell. "Do you name them?"

Harper keeps her eyes trained on her notes. "That would be too many turtles to name."

I nudge her with my elbow. "But you do, don't you?"

"No." The corner of her mouth twitches and I know she's lying.

"Yes, you do. Admit it."

"Travis?"

"What?"

"Shut up."

I turn to protest, but she reaches up and touches her fingers to my lips. I'm not sure what's happening, so I shut up. Harper's hand moves to the back of my neck and pulls my head down until our faces are mere inches apart. "This is probably going to be a mistake," she whispers, before she presses her mouth to mine.

Kissing Harper is different from kissing Paige. For one thing, Harper doesn't taste like Marlboro Lights. I don't have to bend down so far. She fits better against me. And, Jesus, she's a good kisser. So good I want to beat the hell out of whoever taught her.

She's probably right about this being a mistake, but right now? I don't care.

"We, um—we should be watching the turtles." She's breathless and doesn't sound at all convinced. I cast a glance over the edge of the tarp. The first two turtles have left the nest and a third—no, a third and fourth are pushing their way up through the sand.

"We should." The apple scent of her hair tangles around my brain as my lips brush her neck. She shivers in a way that has nothing to do with the temperature, and it pleases me in a way I can't even explain. This time, *I* kiss *her*.

"Travis." The clipboard comes up between us, killing the moment. I don't want to let go, but I do.

"I know." I tap the end of her nose with my finger. "I'll go check on Alpha."

"Alpha?"

"The first turtle," I say. "That's his name."

She beams at me and it's almost enough to make up for the fact that I'm harder than trigonometry right now. Almost.

Chapter 6

It's full-on morning when Harper drops me off at home. Well beyond the sneaking-in hours, past breakfast, and eighty-seven baby sea turtles later. We stopped naming them after Zulu.

"I hope the one we called Juliet is a girl," I say. "Or he's going to have to face the next hundred fifty years being ridiculed by all the other turtles."

She smiles. "Shut up."

I kiss her for the first time since the first time. It doesn't seem strange to me that we spent most of the night not kissing. It's also not jump-in-the-backseat making out. It's just . . . good. Really, really good. "See you later, Charley Harper."

I don't tell her I'll call her, because it would be a cliché. But I already know I will.

"Travis? Is that you?" My mom's voice drifts down from upstairs as I come through the front door. I find her in my room, taking a dark blue thermal shirt from a paper shopping bag. My bed is so thick with bags I can't even see the comforter.

"What's all this stuff?"

"Well, we never went shopping, so I thought I'd pick up a few things for you to wear. I got the sizes from your uniforms." She's babbling, nervous I'm going to hate the things she bought. It's not an unfounded fear. We have history like that. "If there's anything you don't want, I can take it back. And I bought you the shoes we never got around to buying."

"Thanks." I peer into a bag filled with plaid button shirts from one of those pretentious, prewrinkled stores in the mall. Shirts Ryan wears. I could put them on and they'd look fine, but this fake vintage stuff is not me. The last time she bought me clothes from that store, I complained about how it was manufactured in a sweatshop and refused to wear it. That was me back then, spouting statistics I read on the Internet and thinking I was making a difference in the world. "Did you buy the whole mall?"

Relief fills her face and she laughs. "I did go a little overboard, but—I don't know. I just felt as if maybe you wouldn't mind."

"I don't mind," I say. "But if we take some of these clothes back, you could use the money for that school supplies thing you were talking about."

I haven't turned into some rabid do-gooder Boy Scout, but spending seven months living around people who live in mud huts and don't have indoor plumbing has changed my perspective a little. I don't need this much stuff. Especially when I'm going back to Lejeune in a few weeks and then back to Afghanistan next spring.

"That is a very good idea." She holds up the blue thermal and makes a what-do-you-think-of-this-one? face. I nod and she starts removing the tags. "Have you been out all this time?"

"Yeah, I was at the beach with, um—with Harper Gray."

"She's such a sweet girl," Mom says. "I refuse to believe the rumors I heard about her at school."

"What rumors?"

"Mean, vulgar things I don't even want to repeat." She folds the shirt and puts it in a drawer. "I know she runs around with Lacey Ellison and Amber Reynolds, but—well, Harper Gray is not *an* S-L-U-T." She spells it, as if she's offended just saying the word. "What kind of person would even start those kinds of rumors?"

If she only knew.

"An idiot."

"You were at the beach all night?"

"She volunteers with a sea turtle conservation group, so we were monitoring a hatching."

Mom blinks. I'm pretty sure my high school career was more notorious in her mind than in real life. "Really?"

"Yep." I reach into one of the bags and pull out a white T-shirt and a pair of normal-looking cargo shorts. "Do you mind if I borrow the car again? I need to run an errand."

Mom rummages in her purse. "Will you be home for dinner? It'll just be you, me, and Rye."

I give her a grin. "As long as I don't have to cook it."

She laughs and throws me the keys.

After grabbing a quick shower, I head across town.

I had a good time last night with Harper, but the hallucinations and flashbacks are messing with my head. The nightmares suck, too, but at least they've happened when I'm asleep and not a danger to anyone. So far. What if I have a hallucination when I'm driving or something? What if I hurt myself—or worse, someone else?

My cell phone rings and it's Eddie.

"Dude, I bought an AK-47," he says. "Me, Michalski, and Rye are going shooting tomorrow. Wanna come?"

Used to be, every few weeks we'd pile into someone's car and head up to the gun range on Tucker's Grade to release a little 9 mm steam, playing Dirty Harry with Glocks and shotguns and a .38 Special that belonged to Eddie's dad. For Eddie, an AK is a big deal, but everyone in Afghanistan has one. Taliban. The Afghan National Army. Even the farmers, who were mostly Taliban anyway. The novelty wears off after you've been shot at by one, so I'm not all that impressed. But, what the hell. I like shooting stuff. "Yeah, I'm in."

"Where you at?" he asks.

"On my way to a doctor's appointment."

"Everything okay?"

"Yeah," I lie. "Routine checkup."

"Come over later."

"I might," I say as I turn into the parking lot of the veterans' clinic. I feel bad about it, but I don't want to hang out with Eddie tonight.

* * *

I write my name on a sign-in form at the reception desk, but when the receptionist sees that I'm a walk-in patient she shakes one long glittery purple fingernail at me. "It's better to have an appointment." Her accent is Jamaican, or possibly Haitian. "But have a seat"—she looks at the sign-in sheet— "Travis Stephenson, and I will call you as soon as someone is available."

I sit in a red molded plastic chair in a waiting room filled with people who aren't anything like me. There are a couple of regular-looking guys, but they're probably in their thirties or forties. One of them has a prosthetic leg. Straight across the aisle is a wrinkled old veteran in a red Windbreaker with a USS *Saratoga* ball cap and a metal cane. He's thumbing through an old copy of *Newsweek*. His mothball breath blasts across the aisle whenever he coughs. Two seats over from me is a skinny, sketchy-looking guy maybe five years older than me who can't hold still. His knee keeps jittering, shaking the whole row of chairs, and he's missing a couple of teeth.

"You Army?" he asks me, but doesn't wait for my reply. "I was Special Forces. They picked me right out of basic because I already had a black belt in Brazilian jujitsu, so I didn't need much training."

"Hey, good for you, bro," I say, and pick up a back copy of a news magazine that promises an article about the war in Afghanistan, hoping he'll get the hint that I don't want to chat.

"Yeah," he continues. "I led my guys on a whole bunch of covert missions in Africa, and you know when they captured Saddam Hussein? That was us."

"Sure, dude, whatever."

"I'd still be in, but I broke my back on a helo jump," he says. "They weren't sure if I'd ever walk again, but I fought it, you know? The doctors are having trouble getting my meds right, though, because I have to take, like, six pills at once for the pain to even go away."

"Uh-huh." I'm not calling him a liar, but nobody gets picked for Special Forces right out of basic training and he doesn't look old enough to have done everything he claims.

I turn a page in the magazine and discover a series of

photos of my own company, taken by a photographer who'd embedded with us for a few weeks. They're from the beginning of our mission, when we were first deployed and still fairly clean. From when the other guys called Charlie and Kevlar and me FNG—fucking new guy—and Boot. It seems like it was years ago, instead of months.

There's a picture of Kevlar and Charlie waist-deep in a poppy field. The caption only says *US Marines under fire in Helmand Province* and it looks like it could be a picture of any Marines, but I would recognize them anywhere. I turn to the next page and the full-page photo there is of a Marine squatting down on a dusty road, talking to a little Afghan girl who has a tear trickling down her cheek.

It's me.

That day, we were out on patrol and we got mobbed with kids. Little boys mostly, but there was this tiny girl who was knocked down in the stampede. Their grubby, greedy hands waving at me, I pushed my way through the boys to the girl. She was crying—and I hate to see little girls cry. Women, too, but little girls just kill me. When I squatted down, her eyes went huge and afraid, like I was going to hurt her. I guess I can see how she might have thought so, considering I was holding an M16, but instead I gave her a beanbag giraffe. She cradled it in her arms as if I had given her a real live baby, and when she smiled at me, she had a missing front tooth.

The caption turns me into the poster boy for winning

the hearts and minds of the local population, but it doesn't talk about how the Taliban would spread flyers in the night threatening to kill the people if they helped us. Or that a lot of the local population *was* Taliban. The caption makes it look like we made a difference, when I'm not sure that we did.

I'm staring at the picture of myself when the nurse at the check-in desk says my name. "Stephenson? Travis Stephenson."

That Marine right there in the magazine doesn't belong here—at a veterans' clinic with old guys and liars addicted to prescription painkillers. That Marine is hard. That Marine is tough. That Marine is not crazy.

I don't want to sit in some counselor's office every week and talk about how I *feel*, and if Staff Sergeant Leonard, my platoon sergeant, were here right now, he'd tell me to *unfuck* myself and get over it. Guys coming home from France and Germany after World War II, guys coming home from Vietnam . . . they didn't talk about their wars. They didn't see therapists. They filed it away in some tiny, dark corner of their brains and moved on with their lives.

I don't need this.

I roll up the magazine, tuck it into my back pocket, and walk out of the building. Behind me, I hear the receptionist calling my name.

* * *

"So, Trav." Eddie takes the AK-47 from its case and a feeling of cold dread crawls up my spine, freezing me where I stand. I know with every rational bone in my body that my friend is not going to shoot me with that rifle, but my palms are damp and my pulse is racing. My fingers curl into fists, in case I need to punch him, and I wish I had my M16. "I hear you've been hooking up with Harper Gray."

The dread drains away, leaving me nothing but aggravated—at myself for panicking and at Eddie for saying such a stupid thing. "Where'd you hear that?"

"Paige told me you tried to pick up Harper at the Shamrock," Ryan says. "And I saw her come pick you up the other night."

I shrug. "We're friends."

Michalski laughs his big dumb laugh and sticks his face over my shoulder. "Well, she *is* a very friendly girl." He pumps his fist in front of his mouth, simulating a blow job, and I jab my elbow back into his gut. He doubles over, coughing. "Jesus, man, what was that for?"

"Your mouth," I say as Eddie clips a loaded magazine into the rifle and flips the catch. "Keep it shut."

"What is your problem?" Ryan complains. "Everyone knows Harper is a—"

"A *what*?" My tone is knife sharp, and there is no good answer.

"You ladies mind if I go first?" Eddie interrupts, leaving my brother and me glaring at each other. Ryan's fists bunch as if he wants to hit me. As if I'd let him. "I haven't had a chance to fire it yet."

"It's all you," I say.

With Michalski as a buffer between my brother and me, we give Eddie room at the shooting table. I watch through a pair of binoculars as he fires half a magazine at a man-shaped paper target set on a stand about a hundred yards away. *Crack. Crack. Crack.* The sound—sharp and distinctive—is one I heard day after day in Afghanistan and I have to remind myself again that no one is shooting at me.

No one is shooting at me.

Out of fifteen shots, maybe six hit the paper, mostly at the edges. Nothing that would do any permanent damage.

"Damn." Eddie hands the gun to Michalski. "I've heard these things aren't very accurate, but that's just crazy."

I don't point out that it's probably operator error. The insurgent who put a bullet in my best friend didn't seem to have trouble with the accuracy of an AK-47.

Michalski steps up for a turn and empties the remaining fifteen rounds in the magazine, hitting the target only a handful of times. Wounding shots at best. Definitely no fatalities.

"It gets easier," I offer, taking the AK from him. I unclip the empty magazine and replace it with a new one. Ryan flashes me a dirty look, like I'm showing off or something. Like shooting people isn't my job.

"So what's it like?" Eddie asks. "In Afghanistan, I mean."

"Hot and dirty in the summer, cold and dirty in the winter." I can't tell them the things they really want to know. How it feels to kill someone. It's different for everyone, but I felt a rush of adrenaline. A fleeting triumph. And later, in the night when it was quiet, the guilt hit like a sucker punch. Because, even though he was trying to kill me, I'd taken someone's life. These are things I've tried to leave in Afghanistan. Otherwise, how am I ever going to live with myself? "It's a never-ending camping trip from hell."

"Do the chicks really go around completely covered up?" Michalski asks.

We didn't see many women out on the streets, but when we did, they were usually covered in those blue *chadris* that made them look like ghosts. "Pretty much."

Eddie giggles. "You think they leave them on during sex?"

Everyone laughs, easing the tension. I'm smiling as I lean against the shooting table. The AK at my shoulder, I line up the target in my sight. I close my eyes to center myself, then open them.

There's a black-robed Taliban fighter at the other end of the range, standing next to the target. His head is wrapped in a turban with a black scarf hiding the lower portion of his face so only his eyes show. The Muslim version of a Wild West outlaw.

The world seems to slow around me. I can hear my friends laughing and talking, but I don't know what they're saying, and the only thing in focus is that man. The side of his turban is ripped open, the side of his exposed head caked with blood. I know this man.

I killed him.

I try to blink him away, but he won't go. My mouth fills with the salty saliva that comes before you puke, and I have to swallow hard to keep it down.

I squeeze the trigger and the world speeds back up again.

Fifteen rounds later, the dead man is gone and Michalski exhales. "Jesus, Trav." My hands are shaking as I pass the gun to my brother, but I don't think anyone notices. "That was—whoa."

Eddie lowers the binoculars and grins at me. "You are dangerous, dude."

I laugh it off, but I feel very far from dangerous. My heart is pinballing around my chest. Is Kevlar going through this type of shit right now? Or Moss? And if I called them up to ask, would they admit it?

"So this is where the homoerotic male bonding happens," a female voice says.

It's Paige and she's working the Tomb Raider look with a tight olive-green tank top and aviator sunglasses, her hair skimmed back in a ponytail. She looks incredible.

"What are you doing here?" I ask, shoving my hands into my pockets, trying to hide that I'm still shaken. Shak*ing*.

She shrugs. "It's not like this place is a secret."

Michalski's gaze swings to Ryan. "Dude, this is not cool." I don't normally agree with Michalski, but this time he's right. It's always been an unspoken rule that Tucker's Grade is a guy thing. I never would have invited Paige here. "We don't bring girls to the gun range."

"Whatever." Ryan waves him off. "Get over it."

"No, man. Just no," Michalski says. "This is a *thing*. It's our thing and you violated it. The way you snaked your brother's girlfriend while he was in Afghanistan."

It goes quiet in that oh-shit-did-he-really-say-that? sort of way.

"She broke up with him before anything even happened," Ryan protests. "I didn't steal your girlfriend."

He wants to believe that, but I know Paige. And I know my brother. He thinks he's lived his life in my shadow, but you know what? He has no idea how easy he's had it. He's gotten everything he's ever wanted—including Paige—and never had Dad breathing down his neck to be stronger. Faster. Better.

"He's got a point, Rye," I say. "You *are* a thing violator."

I'm talking about inviting Paige to the gun range, but her glossy lips twist into a smug smile. I don't need to see her eyes—shaded behind mirrored lenses—to know she's looking at me. Or what she's thinking.

"Boys." She steps into the fray, pushing between Michalski and Ryan like a referee. "You can take turns peeing on me later." Eddie, who has been fighting not to laugh, chokes on his soda and blows Coca-Cola out his nose. "But I'm here now, so deal with it."

The brown liquid trickling down Eddie's chin cracks all of us up. Except Ryan, who is still mad. I can see it in his shoulders and in the way he shoots. He never once hits the target.

* * *

The nightmare wrenches me awake. The same road. The same bomb. The same helpless despair as I watch Charlie blow up, find myself lying in his place, and then see the Afghan boy leaning over me as I die. Every time it starts I hope this time it will end differently, but it never does.

I know I won't go back to sleep again tonight, so I sit down at my desk, turn on my laptop, and start looking for—and easily finding—photos and videos of my company from the Internet. Some were taken by the embedded reporters who went everywhere with us, others by guys in the unit. There are hundreds of pictures, but I've never seen any of them.

We're all there. Charlie. Clifton "Ski" Kralewski. Moss. Jared "Starvin' Marvin" Perumal. Peralta. Me. There's a picture of Kevlar chasing a goat around the compound that makes me laugh out loud. I remember the day, because Charlie yelled, "Aw, look guys, Kenneth finally found a girl-friend!" and we were so punch-drunk exhausted we laughed until tears were streaming down our faces. The caption on the picture only mentions the boredom that sets in between patrols, not the long debate over whether we should eat the goat.

There's one of my platoon at Camp Bastion before the assault on Marjah. We were all just waiting. Kevlar kept checking and rechecking his rifle, making sure it was lubri-cated. Charlie listened to Bob Marley on his iPod. I pulled my watch cap down over my eyes to block out the light and tried to sleep, even though the anticipation of the unknown was almost unbearable and the guy next to me was snoring.

There's a picture of Ski shaving, his mirror propped on a dirt wall, using bottled water to rinse. He liked to sing when he shaved, but always used the wrong words. The one that always made us laugh the most was when he sang "I'm not big on sausage gravy" in that Garth Brooks low places song.

I'm watching a video of my squad firing on a Taliban sniper position—I remember a bullet skimming just inches over the top of my helmet—when my bedroom door opens.

"Why are you here?" I ask, watching Moss as he darts around the end of a dirt wall and opens fire. It's so weird to see us doing the things we've already done. It's weird that

these moments in time have been captured and people looking at them don't even know that Charlie is dead.

"How'd you know it was me?" Paige's hands slide down
my chest from behind, her Lara Croft ponytail falling over my
shoulder. I hate that she still has this much effect on me.

"You didn't knock." My eyes are on the video until the
last second as she turns my face toward her, and then she's
all lips and tongue and . . . I know I have got to stop doing
this. But I don't.

Charlie was with me the day her letter arrived in a care
package. I let him read it after the other guys had distrib-
uted the porn and cigarettes like Christmas Day. "That's
pretty cold, Solo." Charlie passed me his cigarette and I took
a long drag.

"Yeah," I said. "That's Paige."

"You gonna be okay?" he asked. "Do you need a hug or
something?"

I chuckled a little. "Nah, I'm good."

In-country, I was good. On the other side of the world,
none of the drama could touch me. Now that I'm back and
she's here, I'm not sure how I feel about her. But that's probably because I just got laid and my brain is butter.

"Paige?"

"Hmmm?" She doesn't open her eyes.

"You don't want to get back together, do you?"

"Oh, God, *no*." She laughs softly, making the bed vibrate.
"Is that what you thought?"

"No."

"It's only sex, Travis."

"You think Ryan would think that?" I stand up and pull on my shorts. The need to flee overwhelms me. I don't like who I am with her. This shit has to stop.

"He doesn't have to know."

"Not the point." Rummaging through my desk drawers, I search until I find a blank CD and slide it into my computer. "Why are you in my room right now instead of his?"

"I don't know," she says. "Probably because you never say no."

"Time for you to leave." The laptop drive whirs, burning the downloaded photos onto the disk as I put my T-shirt back on. Paige makes no move to leave. "Now."

"What did the Marines do to you, Trav?" she asks. "You used to be a lot more fun."

I hit the eject and the CD slides out. Slapping my back pocket to make sure my wallet is there, I step barefoot into the new Sambas my mom bought and head for the door.

"Let yourself out," I say. "And don't forget to put the key back where you found it."

I drive to the twenty-four-hour Walgreens up on San Carlos, where they have one of those do-it-yourself photo kiosks. The store is empty except for the cashier, who is sitting on the checkout counter, her tanned legs dangling over the edge. On her feet are a pair of familiar cowboy boots. Lacey Ellison.

We rode the same bus in middle school and I remember her stop was beside a crummy trailer park next to the bridge to Fort Myers Beach. No one wanted to sit beside her because she smelled like pee and Michalski called her FBK— short for Free Breakfast Kid—because she was poor enough to be on the breakfast plan. Back then she used to charge five dollars to make out with her behind the portables. Now she's already starting to look rough and she's barely legal.

"Hey, Lace."

"Travis Stephenson." She hops off the counter and puts her hand in the middle of my chest, all five foot nothing of her blocking my path to the photo machine. "A word."

"Sure."

"Harper told me you went to the beach with her the other night."

"I did," I say. "That a problem?"

"Not yet."

"What are you getting at?"

"She's my friend, Travis," she says. "Amber and me . . . well, Harper isn't the same as us at all, but she doesn't judge. She's the best person I know, and if you break her heart, I will kill you."

I grin at her. "Duly noted, ma'am."

"I'm serious!" She tries to shove me, but she's not strong enough. Her fierce sincerity is cool, though, and I respect it. "Just don't."

I nod. "I won't."

"That's what you say." Lacey lifts herself back onto the counter. "But don't forget what happened the last time she let you kiss her."

A very good point.

She doesn't disturb me while I'm making prints from the downloaded images, but she gives me a free bottle of Coke after about an hour.

"This is broken." She points to a minor indentation on the bottom of the bottle. No sign of leakage. "If you don't drink it, I'm going to have to throw it away."

A little while later, the biker from the Shamrock comes in on his way home from the bar. Lacey hops off the counter with a happy little squeak and launches herself at him. They make out nonstop for about ten minutes, coming up for air only when a customer comes in to buy a pack of Camels and a bag of Doritos.

When I'm finished, she lets me use her employee discount on the stack of finished prints.

"Thank you for shopping at Walgreens," she deadpans, then points her finger at me. "Remember what I said."

She flicks her eyes toward her biker boyfriend and that means I'm supposed to be scared. I could take him in a fight, but I guess that's really not the point. "I will."

I'm not ready to go home yet, so I drive out to the Waffle House to see if Harper is working. The waitress behind the counter tells me it's her day off and I'm a little disappointed. I order a cup of coffee to go.

"Are you stalking me again?" Harper shoulder-bumps me as she comes up beside me at the counter. She's wearing a black Social Distortion T-shirt with a pair of faded red shorts. I used to have a shirt just like it, but hers looks better.

"I was here first. So who's doing the stalking now?"

"Don't flatter yourself, Stephenson," she says. "I came to get paid."

I wait as she disappears behind the door to the office. She's back in less than a minute with her paycheck in hand. After I pay for my coffee, I walk her out to the Land Rover.

"So what are you doing today?" she asks, leaning against the car door as if she's in no hurry to leave. I'm getting all kinds of crazy good signals from her.

"Coffee, nap, and then my day is wide open," I say. "Why? Are you asking me out?"

"In your dreams."

I laugh. "If my dreams were about you, Harper, it would make sleeping a whole lot more appealing."

Her cheeks go pink. "What does that mean?"

"Nothing." I step into the space between us and take her face in my hands. I kiss her for days. Or maybe just a couple of minutes. It's hard to tell. The phone in her hip pocket vibrates against my leg and she laughs against my mouth and says she has to go.

"Do you want to do something tonight?" I ask.

She gets into the Land Rover and shuts the door. For a moment I think she's blowing me off, but then she rolls down the window. "Yes."

* * *

Paige is gone when I get home, and my mom and Ryan are still asleep. In my room, I shuffle through the stack of photos until I find my favorite. It's of Charlie and me playing rock-paper-scissors to decide which of us would be first to read the latest-to-us issue of *Playboy*. In the picture, he's throwing rock while I'm throwing scissors and losing my shot at Miss March. Rock-paper-scissors was the way we decided everything, and it's only now I realize Charlie almost always threw rock. Using a stray thumbtack from the back of my night-stand drawer, I pin the photo to the wall beside the bed.

It looks random and strange. It doesn't belong on this wall of concert flyers and band posters. As quietly as possible, I drag my bed away from the wall and tear down everything, until the picture is the only thing left. Then I go downstairs to the kitchen.

Dad is standing at the sink in sweatpants, drinking bottled water and looking out the window at the Caloosahatchee.

"What are you doing?" There is accusation in his tone. As if searching the kitchen junk drawer for thumbtacks is on his list of unacceptable behavior.

"What are *you* doing?" I fling the accusation back. "I thought Mom kicked you out."

"It's really none of your concern, Travis," he says. "And, frankly, this prodigal son act is wearing thin."

"It's not an act."

"By the way." Dad caps the bottle and puts it back in the refrigerator. "I'm not sure your brother would appreciate hearing about these late-night visits from Paige. So how about you stay out of my business and I stay out of yours."

Fuck.

As I climb the stairs back to my room, it takes everything in me not to turn around and punch that smug smile off his face. Instead, I pin up all the photos—243 of them—until the wall is covered with little windows back to a place and time when I didn't feel so untethered.

When I'm finished, it doesn't look nice. The rows are crooked and Dad will lose his shit when he sees 243 pinholes in his precious walls. I thought it was going to make me feel better, but it doesn't.

I crash out on my bed.

Just before I close my eyes, I see Charlie sitting on my chair.

"Go away, Charlie," I say. "I'm not in the mood for this shit right now."

He doesn't say anything and he doesn't go away. He just sits there staring at me.

"Go the fuck away!" I shout, and wing my pillow as

hard as I can at him. It hits the lamp on my desk, knocking it to the floor. The bulb shatters and the shade crumples.

My door flies open. Mom rushes in, her arms waving frantically. "Is everything all right? I heard a crash. Are you hurt?"

"Go away." I'm not sure if I'm talking to her or Charlie, but he's gone now and she starts picking up shards of broken bulb, placing them gently into her palm.

"Travis, your dad—"

She wants to offer some sort of explanation, but there is nothing she can say that I want to hear.

"I don't want to talk about this. At all." I roll toward the wall, listening as she wordlessly cleans up the glass. If she notices the wall, she doesn't mention it. I pretend I'm asleep until she leaves.

Chapter 7

Harper is wearing a purple halter top thing that sparkles and she did that magic trick girls do to make her wavy hair straight, and as I walk her to my new Jeep I can't stop staring. It's not because she's hot—I mean, she always is. But normally she's girl-next-door-in-a-neighborhood-where-I-want-to-live hot. Tonight? She's incredible and I'm glad I wore a button shirt.

"Is this yours?" she asks.

When I woke up this morning I found a note on the counter telling me I am no longer allowed to drive my mom's Suburban because I'm not covered by their insurance. Which is just my dad's passive-aggressive way of punishing me. The note also said I need to patch the pinholes in my room before I go back to Lejeune. Like I actually will.

I took a cab up to Palm Beach Boulevard, which is lined with mom and pop–type car dealerships offering the cleanest cars, lowest prices, and onsite financing, and had the driver drop me off at the first place on the strip. I bought a black Jeep from a tired-looking salesman who gave me a couple hundred off the price for paying in cash. It's nothing special, but it's a set of wheels.

"Yep," I say. "I bought it today. Just for you."

"Shut up." She laughs and backhands me in the stomach. This is the girl I recognize.

"So, I was thinking, um—movie?" I have no idea what I'm doing. Paige and I didn't exactly go out on dates. We hooked up. Her house. My house. In the car. On the beach. At parties. With Harper, I'm treading new ground.

"Sounds good."

"Sorry about the top." I'd taken the soft cover off the Jeep when I got it home, but now I'm regretting it. "It'll probably—your hair looks really—good. I mean, not that it doesn't usually. Jesus, I suck at this."

"At what?"

"This whole date thing." I run my hand over my head. "I should have left the top on."

I'm embarrassed and I'm not sure why. Maybe because she throws me off my game. Maybe because when it comes to Harper Gray, I feel like I have no game.

She leans across the gear box and kisses my cheek. "It's only hair."

"Play some music," I say, starting the engine. Letting Paige choose was always dicey because she has lousy taste. But Harper picks Flogging Molly and soon we're driving up 41, singing along as if this isn't a first date, and we get to the movie theater way too quick.

I pull into a parking spot and look over at her. "Your hair is a mess."

She sticks her tongue out at me, then turns my rearview mirror in her direction and brushes her hair back into place.

"What do you want to see?" she asks as we wait in the ticket line.

"I have no idea what's even playing," I say. I don't remember the last time I saw a movie that wasn't on the tiny screen of Charlie's iPod. "I'm up for anything, I guess. Except a chick movie."

"Action?"

One of the NOW PLAYING posters advertises one about an Army platoon in Iraq and I want to see it. Only I'm afraid of what might happen in the theater. I'm not even sure about seeing an action movie because who knows if the sound of gunshots is going to set me off again? I hate that my options have been reduced to chick flicks and comedies.

"How about this one?" I point to the military film.

Skepticism registers on Harper's face before she smiles. "Okay."

It's good she's game, but it sucks she's thinking the same thing I'm thinking. That she even has to think it.

"Popcorn?" I ask, after I buy the tickets.

"Dude." She looks at me as if I'm out of my mind. "Why would you even need to ask that? Popcorn is a given."

"One popcorn," I tell the guy behind the snack counter. "Two Cokes—oh, wait." I look at Harper. "Coke okay? Or diet?"

"No diet."

"Candy?"

"Skittles."

"My favorite."

Skittles come in some of the MREs and most everyone loves them because they don't melt in the heat and they aren't bad luck, like Charms. No one has ever told me why those are bad luck, only that Marine superstition says so.

We pick seats near the middle.

The movie opens with Humvees rolling through the desert, past a small hamlet where a little girl wearing a red hijab waves at them. One of the soldiers waves back and seconds later an airstrike hits the buildings right behind her.

Fuck.

My heart rate spikes.

Fuck.

Why did I think this was a good idea?

Fuck.

I have to get out of here.

"This isn't going to work." I stand up and maneuver myself around people's knees to the end of the row. Down the steps. Out the door. Into the well-lit hallway, where I lean over and try to catch my breath. A few minutes later, Harper comes out of the theater, her arms overflowing with the popcorn, sodas, and candy. "Oh, shit, I'm sorry," I say. I take the drinks out of her hands, even though mine are shaking.

She smiles. "I'm a waitress, remember? It's all good."

A wave of anger crashes over me. At myself for being unable to control my reactions. At Harper for just putting on a smile and saying it's all good when it's *not* all good. I throw my soda cup at the wall. It bursts on impact, splashing Coke everywhere.

"You're too fucking nice to me." I'm yelling at her and I don't know why.

"What do you want me to do, Travis?" she yells back. "Be mad at you about *this*? Don't be stupid."

I drop down onto a bench, my head in my hands. "I'm sorry."

Harper sits down and leans against me. Her comfort moves through me from where her body touches mine, and it makes me feel better.

"I should have known," I say.

"Probably," she agrees. "We can see something else. How do you feel about monsters?"

She points across the hallway to the theater, where an animated kids' film is playing, and raises her eyebrows. I look around. We're alone. No one to catch us if we switch theaters. I grin. "On three—"

Harper laughs, but we don't sneak. We just pick up the snacks and walk into the other theater. The previews are still playing, so we haven't missed anything. We try again, picking seats near the middle.

The tension in my body is gone as I reach over the armrest and take Harper's hand in mine. "Thanks."

She doesn't look away from the screen as she smiles. "Shut up and eat your popcorn."

But she also doesn't let go of my hand. Even when the movie is over.

Chapter 8

A couple days later I awake and find myself unable to get out of bed. Literally. I can barely lift my arms and legs beneath the sheet, and it feels as if something is holding me down. Panic spreads through me and I wonder if this is some new thing wrong with me. It's not bad enough my brain plays tricks on me, now my body isn't cooperating?

"Mom!" I call out. I can't reach my cell phone or even push off the covers.

My bedroom door swings open and a deep voice says, "Your mama can't help you now, boy."

Jesus Christ, I think I'm dying.

I lift my head and C. J. Moss is standing in the doorway with Kevlar doubled over laughing in the hall behind him.

"What the fuck did you do to me?"

They come giggling into the room and I hope whatever they've done is not duct-tape related. That will hurt. Kevlar strips off the sheet with a flourish. Crisscrossing my body is a network of a couple dozen bungee cords, holding me in place. I want to be pissed, but I can't, because Kevlar has this high-pitched giggle that makes it impossible not to laugh.

"I thought I was having a fucking stroke," I say as they free me from my coated elastic prison, making them laugh even harder. "What are you doing here?"

"I was bored." Kevlar packs a pinch of dip while I pull on a pair of shorts. "So I called up Moss over there and said, 'C. J., my man, it's time for a road trip.'"

Moss rolls his eyes. He doesn't talk much. Of course, you don't really need to talk when Kevlar won't shut up. I can't even imagine that road trip.

"So we jumped in the truck and here we are," Kevlar says. "Let's have some fun!"

"What time is it?" I peek between the blinds. "Jesus, Kenny, it's still dark outside."

"I choose to see it as a preemptive strike on the day." He rubs his hands together like he's starting a fire. "C'mon, Solo, time's a-wastin'."

"What do you want to do?" I yank on a T-shirt and start making my bed.

"I say we—" Kevlar starts to speak, but Moss clamps a hand over his mouth. "I want to go deep-sea fishing," he says. "I remember you talking about that, Solo. I want to catch fish."

"Done."

"I was thinking more like hot girls in bikinis and body shots—oh, hello again, Mrs. Stephenson," Kevlar says as my mom comes into the room. We really haven't talked much since Dad moved back home, and I feel uncomfortable around her again. I don't want things to be this way between us—she was really cool for a while—but I don't think she wants to hear what I have to say. And vice versa.

"Thanks for aiding and abetting their mission, Mom," I say. "They strapped me to my bed with bungee cord."

She laughs. "I came up to see if your friends will be spending the night."

"Thank you for your generosity, ma'am," Kevlar says. "But we've already booked a room down on the beach."

"We should probably get going," I say.

"Where are you boys off to at such an early hour?" Mom asks.

"Fishing."

"Oh, that should be fun." The enthusiasm in her voice doesn't match the sadness in her eyes. "Will you be around for dinner?"

"We'll probably go out."

"Okay, well, be sure to take sunscreen." She follows us down the stairs, and when I shut the front door behind us, it feels like the day we left our outpost in Marjah. There were dogs that hung around our camp and even though we weren't supposed to feed them, we did. When we left for the last time, this one white dog with black spots on his ears stood there looking hopeful—as if maybe we wouldn't leave. That's how my mom looks now and it makes me feel bad.

"Can we get some breakfast?" Moss asks as we pile into the Jeep. Kevlar calls shotgun.

"We can stop somewhere," I say. "What do you want?"

"Waffle House."

"Not again," Kevlar groans at Moss's suggestion. "Solo, did you know there are thirty-eight Waffle Houses between here and Lejeune? Now, we haven't eaten in *all* of them, but wouldn't you say four in a seventeen-hour period is excessive?"

"I *like* Waffle House," Moss says.

Harper is probably working, which is a good enough reason for me. "Shut up, Kenneth. If the man wants Waffle House, we're going to Waffle House."

* * *

Harper looks up as we enter the restaurant. Kevlar is out in front, so I wink at her and put my finger to my lips. She gives us a bright, generic smile. "Hi! Welcome to Waffle House. Have a seat anywhere and I'll be right with you."

"Damn, Solo, if there were girls who looked like that in

the other Waffle Houses, I'd have stopped at every single one of them," Kevlar says.

"Why? So you could sit there and not talk to them the way you did when you, me, and Charlie went to New York?"

"Shut the fuck up."

"C. J.," I say, "you should have seen him. The whole trip he talked about how he was going to get laid. Then we get to the bars and he's like, 'She's hot. Maybe I'll go ask her to dance.' And Charlie and I would be all, 'Do it.' But did he? No."

"I talked to that one girl."

"Oh, that's right." I nod. "*One* girl. Did you get laid? Kiss her? Get her phone number? Dude, it's not difficult. In fact, I bet I can get that girl"—I point at Harper—"to kiss me before breakfast is over."

"No way." Kevlar shakes his head. "You're not *that* good."

"How much?"

"Twenty bucks," he says.

"Deal."

Harper brings menus and silverware. "My name is Harper. Can I get you some coffee? Or maybe some orange juice?"

"Harper? That's a *beautiful* name," I say. "Were you named after Harper Lee?"

The corner of her mouth twitches, but she doesn't give anything away. "No, Charley Harper."

"The artist? He's one of my favorites," I say. "My name's Travis and these are my friends Kenny—"

"Ken," he interrupts, and I nearly lose it. Ken? Since when? "Ken Chestnut."

"And this is C. J."

"Very nice to meet you," she says. "You gentlemen aren't from around here, are you?"

"We're down for a couple of days from North Carolina," I say.

"Marines," Kevlar adds. "We just got back from Afghanistan."

She turns her high-beam smile on him and his face goes as red as his hair. "Nice."

"We're going deep-sea fishing later," I say. "You wouldn't—would you like to join us?"

Then she smiles at me and this charade takes on a whole new dimension and I like it. A lot. "Sure, sounds fun," Harper says. "Now, about those drinks."

While she's gone, Kevlar fills me in on company gossip. I don't know how he finds it all out, but he has dirt on nearly everyone. "Dude, you remember Nardello from second platoon? His wife left him and took everything, even his '66 Mustang."

"Damn, that's cold."

"And Day—dude, he tried to off himself."

"What? No."

"Yeah," Kevlar says. "He was pretty tight with Palmer."

Palmer was one of the eight from our battalion who were killed. I didn't know Day or Palmer very well, but I guess I know how Day feels. Like you're a glass that's filled to the top. Then you have to face everything back home and the glass overflows.

Harper comes back with a pot of coffee and I push it all out of my mind. "You guys know what you want?"

Moss orders biscuits and gravy with grits and Kevlar goes for a pecan waffle, but I cock my head and look up at her. "All I want is a kiss."

Her eyebrows lift. "What?"

"Nothing on the menu would compare."

Kevlar groans and even I have to admit it's the cheesiest thing I have ever said. But this isn't about successful pickup lines. It's about winning twenty bucks from the guy who bungee-corded me to my bed.

"Well, that's just about the sweetest thing I've ever heard," she says, and slides into the booth beside me. Harper touches my face with her fingertips and presses her lips against mine. She smells like apples and bacon and maple syrup. This is supposed to be a joke, but her tongue teasing against mine makes the Waffle House disappear and sends me dangerously close to cold shower territory. Her green eyes are on mine as she pulls slowly away and gives me a tiny, private smile. I extend my hand across the table—palm up—and Kevlar slaps a twenty in it. Harper gives me another quick peck on the lips, then stands up. "Are you having the usual, Travis?"

"Yep."

"Solo, man, that was so not fair," Kevlar protests.

I snap the bill between my fingers. "I'd say it *almost* makes us even."

Moss laughs and fist-bumps me, and I feel the most normal I've felt since the day we got back from Afghanistan—except for when I'm alone with Harper. These are my brothers. This is my family.

"Hey, Harper?" I call across the restaurant.

"Yeah?"

"I was serious about the fishing."

"Me, too," she says. "I just have to finish up with this table of idiot Marines and I'll be ready."

"So, wait. Are you and her . . . ?" Kevlar's head swivels from me to Harper and back. He leaves the thought unfinished, which sums up me and Harper pretty accurately. Unfinished. She's not my girlfriend, but I'm not interested in anyone else. Unless you count Paige, but . . . I don't know why she gets to me the way she does. I don't like her the way I like Harper. He drops his head to the table, making the silverware rattle. "This world is so unfair."

"Dude," I say. "I told you already. If you're going to get a girl, you have to actually talk to one."

He gives me the finger without looking up.

Harper finishes her shift and we follow her to the radio station, where she leaves the Rover for her dad. Driving down Daniels, Kevlar keeps rocking forward in the passenger's seat, as if he's trying to make the Jeep go faster.

"Jesus, Solo," he complains. "My old granny drives faster than you."

"I'm doing sixty." The limit is forty-five and I'm keeping pace with traffic. "What's your rush?"

Moss leans through the space between the seats. "You should have seen him on the drive down," he says. "We'd have been here even earlier if he didn't get stopped three times for speeding. Boy has some serious road rage, too. Shit. I'm less afraid of the Taliban than his cracker-ass driving."

I laugh, but I can't help wondering if this is what Kevlar brought home from Afghanistan. And what about Moss? He told me that he grew up in the projects in Baltimore. He wasn't a gang member and he wasn't from a single-mother home. His dad was ex-Army on disability and they couldn't afford a better neighborhood. Moss told me once he plans to go to college when he gets out next year.

"Seeing people get killed is nothing new for me, Solo," he said to me once, while we were lifting weights in our makeshift patrol base gym. "You do what you can to let it go. Otherwise it'll eat you up."

I glance at him in the rearview mirror and he's looking at the scenery as we pass, all Buddha-serene. Maybe he's the lucky one.

* * *

Kevlar reminds me of a dog with his head stuck out the window as our charter captain, Gary, speeds the boat across the water, heading for fish. Kevlar's got a beer in his hand and the go-fast he's been craving. For the first time since they showed up at my bedroom door, he looks really relaxed.

Moss is in the cabin, looking a little seasick.

"Do my back?" Harper—stripped down to a green-striped bikini top and shorts—hands me a bottle of sunscreen. The bruise she gave me below my eye is still fading to yellow, but she's inviting me to touch her bare skin. It's kind of a mind-fuck moment and I have to mentally field strip an M16 to keep from getting turned on—but I like it.

Kevlar comes into the cabin for another beer as I'm spreading the sunscreen between her shoulders. His red eyebrows lift over the top edge of his sunglasses and he mouths *son of a bitch* at me, making me laugh. "Anyone else want a beer?"

Moss shakes his head. He still looks a little queasy.

"Too early for me," I say.

"Dude, it's happy hour in Helmand." Kevlar throws me a beer, which nearly slides out of my sunscreen-covered hand. I touch the can to Harper's back, making her squeak. As she turns around to smack my arm, I watch Kevlar chug his entire beer, then go back to the fridge for another.

"Travis?" I turn to look at Harper. Her voice goes quiet. "Everything okay?"

I'm not sure how to answer. I have my own shit. I'm not sure I can deal with his, too. But maybe I should. Maybe that's what we need—to talk about Afghanistan, about

Charlie. There's a dot of sunscreen at the tip of her nose, so I reach up and rub it in. "Yeah, I'm good." I don't think she believes me. "Give me and Kevlar a minute?"

"Dude, you okay?" I ask, after Harper is back out on deck.

"Yeah, why?" Kevlar says.

"I don't know. Just seems like you're drinking a lot."

"The hell, Solo?" His eyebrows pull together and he frowns. "I'm on *vacation*."

"Sorry, man." I throw up my hands. "I'm just saying if you need to talk or whatever—"

"Fuck off." Kevlar goes back out on deck, facing into the wind. The boat hits a wave and a spray of salt water catches him in the face. He lets out a joyous whoop, grinning like a fool.

I go out beside Moss. "How long has he been this way?"

"Since we got home, I guess," he says. "I took the bus to see my family, so I'm not sure. On the way down here he told me he spent a night in jail back home in Tennessee for getting in a bar fight. I don't know, Solo. It's like real life isn't big enough for him anymore."

Chapter 9

It's a calm day on the water, so the waves aren't too big. Moss seems to have found his sea legs—and a beer.

"I'm catching a shark today," Kevlar announces as Gary distributes the fishing rods. We're trolling on a school of tarpon, but Gary says there's a chance we could see some sharks. "A black tip or a lemon—or a *hammerhead*," Kevlar says. "Yeah, a hammerhead would be sweet."

He pivots the fishing rod back, about to cast, when Gary stops him. "Slow down, son, you're not going to catch anything without *bait*."

"Except a buzz," Moss says.

"Nah," I say. "He's already caught one of those."

Kevlar gives us the finger, while Gary uses a live

pilchard—bait fish—to bait the hook for him. Harper baits her own.

I move up behind her, my mouth next to her ear and my hand on her hip. The sunscreen makes her smell like summertime. "You are officially the coolest girl in the world."

She shivers, but plays it off by rolling her eyes at me. "You're just now figuring that out?"

"I've had my suspicions."

Harper turns to face me and places her hands on my chest. I ignore the fact that they're covered in fish slime because, well—it's Harper. And she's going to kiss me. "Travis?"

"Yeah?"

"Go away." She gives me a shove. "I have a shark to catch."

Kevlar cracks up. "Ooh, Solo. *Denied*."

"Hey, Kenneth, aren't you going to introduce me to your date?" I reach into the live well and pull out a pilchard for my own hook. "Oh, wait. You don't *have* one."

He takes a long drink, then burps. "Harper could set us up with a couple of her friends."

As I cast my line, I consider hooking Kevlar up with Lacey Ellison. He could finally get laid. I glance at Harper.

"Don't even think it," she says, not taking her eyes off the water. "I have no control over what my friends do with random guys they meet in bars, but I'm not pimping them out to the Marine Corps."

This makes me laugh. "I guess that's fair."

Today is a good day. Sunshine. Beer. Fishing. And Afghanistan is as far away as it belongs. I don't need therapy. I just need more days like this.

Moss catches the first fish, a flashing silver tarpon that lights him up with happiness. They're great game fish, tarpon, but not much for eating, so Gary takes a picture of Moss holding up his catch before they release it back into the Gulf.

"Solo?" Moss asks, casting out a fresh line. "They have these kinds of fish up in North Carolina?"

"Sure," I say. "We can go anytime you want, man."

He gives me that Buddha smile. "Cool."

"I've got something," Harper says, a little while later, when the line on her reel starts peeling off fast. The muscles in her arm flex as she tries to crank it in and I can tell it's something big.

"Tarpon," Gary says, but she shakes her head.

"It seems like it's going deeper," she says. "Maybe a shark?"

"Well, then sit down in the fishing chair," he says. "And hang on."

Whatever she's hooked into is running. It's not like in the cartoons, when the fish takes off swimming and the boat goes zipping along behind it. But sharks are strong and the boat starts pointing in the direction of whatever is on the other end of Harper's line.

After a couple of minutes the drag stops spinning and Harper starts cranking it in. She's strong, but the pressure on the rod is pretty intense.

"You doing okay?" I ask.

"Yeah," she says. The loose hairs escaped from her ponytail are damp and sticking to the back of her neck. "I could use some water."

Kevlar brings her a bottle, and to keep the sun out of her face I give her an old Brewers ball cap I got when we lived in Green Bay.

With the boat following Harper's shark, Kevlar has to settle for cooler fishing, which doesn't bother him at all. He's already half in the bag. Moss, on the other hand, is content to watch Harper fish. Like he's committing it all to memory.

For about thirty minutes it goes like this: the drag peels off as the shark runs, taking as much line with it as it can; the drag stops and Harper reels in, taking back as much of the line as she can. It's tedious and her arms tremble from the effort.

"Do you want some help?" I offer.

"No." She gives me a grim smile. "But thanks."

It's no surprise she turns me down; she's probably better at fishing than I am, anyway. And that's kind of hot.

Forty-five minutes, maybe an hour, pass before the shark starts getting as tired as Harper. In the shade of the Brewers cap, she's fighting not to cry, and part of me wants to take the pole away to give her a break, but she's too stubborn for that. One step forward, two steps back, she slowly reels it in. The drag zings out each time the shark thrashes against her, trying to throw the hook, and she struggles to gain it back.

Then—like in the last second of an arm wrestling match where the weaker of the two gives up—the shark just stops fighting. Harper makes up a yard, then two, then ten.

"Looks like it's done," Gary says. "But beware, it may start thrashing again when it gets to the boat."

At first the shark is only a dark shadow deep in the water and we can't tell what it is, but as it gets closer to the surface we can see the distinct shape of a hammerhead. And it's a monster.

"Jesus," Kevlar breathes. "How are we going to get that thing on the boat?"

"That fish is ten, possibly twelve feet long, son," Gary says. "It's not coming on this boat." He turns to Harper. "Keep reeling."

The hammerhead breaks the surface and goes nuts, thrashing and flailing, churning up the water around it. I look back at Harper and grin. "You've got him." The corners of her mouth curl up a little, but it's hard to tell if she's smiling or grimacing as she tries to beat the last bit of fight the shark has left. Finally, he surrenders and lies over on his side, just floating there. Spent. One end of his ugly head sticks up out of the water, his beady black eye looking almost bewildered. Like he's wondering what the hell just happened.

Kevlar leans over the side and touches the shark. "That is so fucking cool."

"If you want a picture, now is the time," Gary says. "And make it quick because we need to let it go."

Moss takes the rod from Harper so I can snap a picture with the camera on my phone. Gary hands her a pair of clippers to cut the wire leader that will set the hammerhead free. There's no way to pull the hook out from between those razor teeth. It will stay there until it rusts away. "Do you want to name it? Some people like to do that."

"No, that's okay." Harper snips the leader and the shark slowly swims away, his dorsal fin sinking below the water before the fish disappears completely.

"That was awesome." I move beside her and slip my arm around her waist. Her whole body is quivering with exhaustion as she leans into me, closing her eyes. I kiss her forehead and it's damp with sweat.

* * *

After fishing a couple more hours—Harper went into the cabin and slept the whole time—we drop Kevlar and Moss at their hotel, then drive up the island to her house.

"I'll give you the grand tour," she says as I follow her onto the front porch. "It won't take long, since you can stand in the living room and see everything."

Harper throws open the door and stops in her tracks. I crash into her from behind, grabbing her around the waist to keep from knocking her down. On the couch, just over her shoulder, Harper's dad and a dark-haired woman are making out. They jump apart, fumbling with their tangled clothes. Her lip gloss is smeared at the side of his mouth and they look so . . . busted.

"Okay, this is embarrassing," her dad says as they stand. They're holding hands. "Harper, this is Alison Redding. Alison, this is Harper and her friend Travis."

"Not exactly how I envisioned this moment." Alison's smile is bright, genuine, as she reaches out to Harper, who is immobile within the circle of my arm. I'm not sure she's even breathing. "But it's nice to finally meet you."

Harper doesn't say anything. She breaks away from me and goes into her room, slamming the door. Leaving me holding the big bag of awkward.

Her dad blows out a breath and scratches the back of his head. "I should go talk to her."

"It would probably be better if you didn't," I say. "Let me."

"I don't think . . ." He glances at her door, as if I'd try something with his daughter right now, then he sighs. "Yeah, okay."

I tap on Harper's door. "Hey, it's me."

Her face appears in the open crack, her eyes damp.

"Can I come in?"

She opens the door wider and I'm in her bright yellow

room, standing beside her bed. I have to admit, my preferred course of action would be to drag her beneath the blankets and do things that would take her mind off her dad. Except that's not what she wants right now. And considering everything I've put her through, it won't kill me to shut up and listen.

"When he told me she was thinking about coming to visit, I thought that meant they were, you know, talking about a future visit." Harper drops down on her bed. "I didn't think it meant *now*, like . . . *that*."

I sit beside her and look around the room. Hanging on the walls are brightly colored paintings of cartoon-like sea creatures. Red turtles. Purple seahorses. Green goldfish. Orange dolphins. They're kind of cool. I wonder if Harper's mom painted them. "Who is she?"

"They were engaged." She rubs her eyes on the back of her hand. I offer her the sleeve of my fish-scented T-shirt and she turns her face into my shoulder. "He broke it off when he met my mom."

I suck at this. Being a guy is way less complicated sometimes. "Maybe, um, you should talk to him?"

"No. I'm not ready." She wipes her eyes on my sleeve. "Let's just stick to our plans."

"Okay."

She opens her bottom dresser drawer and hands me a red towel. "There's a shower out back with soap and shampoo.

Be sure to close the curtain all the way or the old woman across the canal will call the sheriff."

"Sounds exciting."

I'm reaching for the doorknob when she crosses the small room and pins me against the door, kissing me the way she did at the Waffle House this morning. Damn.

We're both a little breathless when she pulls away.

"Thank you, Travis."

Her dad and Alison are waiting at the kitchen table as I pass through, the red towel strategically placed to hide wood. He nearly knocks the chair over as he stands up. I can't even imagine a dad who cares the way Harper's does. "Is she okay?"

"She's mostly confused."

"I was kind of hoping Harper would join us for sushi," he says. "So she can get to know Alison."

"I wouldn't." I don't tell him the image of them making out is probably still burned onto her retinas. "She thought this was a theoretical someday event. She needs some time to wrap her head around it."

"Thanks, Travis." He shakes my hand. "You're a good man."

I doubt he'd say that if he knew I was on my way to take a cold shower.

Chapter 10

A mountain of broken crab legs, empty oyster shells, and peeled-away shrimp skins rises up in the middle of a table on the hotel balcony overlooking the Gulf. We've eaten a ton of seafood we had delivered from Pincher's Crab Shack, and if the number of Corona bottles with squeezed-up limes at the bottom is any indication, we've killed a case of beer. We're all a little sunburned and more than a little drunk. I wonder why Kevlar has not passed out yet.

"The night is young and downstairs is a bar full of young, nubile women." He comes out of the bathroom wearing a plaid cowboy shirt and jeans so new I wonder if the tags are still attached.

"Look at you," I say. "Going to the rodeo there, Kenneth?"

"Damn straight." He grins. "Gonna find me a woman, grab on, and—" He bucks his hips like he's riding a bull and waves his cowboy hat in the air. "Woo-hoo!"

Moss laughs. "My money says you don't last the full eight seconds."

I hit him with a fist bump.

"Fuck you guys," Kevlar says. "Tonight's the night. I can feel it. Who's in?" I glance at Harper, and he groans. "Solo, I never expected these words to ever come out of my mouth, but you, my friend, are whipped."

I point my beer bottle at him, squinting one eye as if I'm aiming. "Don't make me come over there and kick your ass."

"I'm just sayin'."

"Yeah, well, let's examine the facts, shall we?" I say. "I am here with a girl, who happens to be insanely hot"—Harper goes pink—"while you are dressed like a Tennessee douchebag in the hopes of possibly getting some trim. Harper could turn me down tonight, tomorrow night, and the night after that, and I'd *still* have a better chance of getting laid, you inbred hilljack."

We glare at each other until Kevlar cracks a smile and then starts giggling. Soon all of us are cracking up, except Harper, who looks mystified.

"You guys are so mean to each other," she says, which only makes us laugh harder.

It's true. We say the most offensive stuff to each other.

Racist. Homophobic. Insulting each other's moms. Sometimes, every once in a while, it leads to knock-down-roll-around-on-the-ground fistfights, but mostly we laugh because we don't mean it. Any one of us would take a bullet for the other.

"So are we partying or what?" Kevlar asks, packing some Skoal in his lower lip.

Moss shrugs. "I'm in."

"Yep," Harper says.

Kevlar tries to drape his arm around her shoulders as we walk down the hall to the elevator, but it's kind of difficult considering she's about four inches taller than him. "You know," he says, "it ain't too late to kick Solo to the curb."

"Why do you guys call him that?" she asks.

"You know how in *Star Wars*, just before the garbage masher walls are about to start closing in, Han Solo goes, 'I got a bad feeling about this'?"

Harper nods.

"Well, it's pitch-black night in the 'Stan," Kevlar says. "And we're boarding helos that are going to drop us in the middle of West Bumfuck, where God knows who is going to be shooting at us, and out of the blue Stephenson goes, 'I got a bad feeling about this.'"

"We were scared shitless," Moss adds. "But every time one of us would repeat it, we'd start laughing all over again."

I remember the nightmare feeling when the helos left us there in the black unknown, covered in our first layer of dirt, unable to walk away. Unable to change our minds and go home.

My joke wasn't prophetic. We raided a couple of houses, rounded up a handful of suspected bad guys, and by the time the sun came up, we felt like cowboys—and I was permanently Han Solo.

I move between Kevlar and Harper, putting my arm around her.

"They also call me Solo," I say against her neck, making her shiver, "because I always get the girl."

She side-eyes me. "Han Solo was kind of a tool."

Kevlar giggles and spits tobacco juice into the mouth of an empty beer bottle. "She does have a point."

"He's the one who ran interference against the Empire so Luke Skywalker could blow up the Death Star," I protest. "He's a hero."

"He's a scoundrel." Harper smirks at me as she presses the down button beside the elevator doors, and I smile back because she knows her *Star Wars*.

"You like me because I'm a scoundrel," I say, quoting the movie. "There aren't enough scoundrels in your life."

The elevator dings and the doors slide open. Harper looks at me, then at Moss, then at Kevlar—and laughs. "So not true."

The club downstairs is surprisingly full for August. Only none of the women here are young or nubile. It's full of middle-aged people in tropical clothes, rocking out—if you can even call it that—to a Jimmy Buffett tribute band called the Floridays.

"Lots of fine, fine ladies here tonight, Kenneth," I say. "Which one's it going to be?"

"If I wanted a cougar, I'd do your mom."

"Why? Getting tired of your own?"

He ignores me. "This place sucks. Where else can we go?"

We walk to the Shamrock.

Harper's friends are in residence at a table near the bar. Lacey squeals and makes an instant beeline in our direction, her cowboy boots tapping on the floor as she walks. I glance at Kevlar to see if he's checking out her tiny denim skirt, but his eyes are locked on Amber, whose hair is now dyed a shade of red a lot like . . . his.

"Dude, no." She's Tour de France. He's training wheels. He's so not ready for Amber Reynolds.

"Dude, yes," he says.

"Harper! Travis!" Lacey reaches for us, pulling us to her table, but her smile is directed at . . . Moss? Not that I have a problem with that, because he's good-looking for, you know, a *guy*. It's just that this is not the way I expected it would go down, if it went down at all. "So are you going to introduce us to your friends?"

I make the introductions, then head to the bar and order a pitcher of beer. While the bartender is pouring, I look back at the table, where Lacey curls herself around Moss's bicep and a nervous-looking Kevlar is talking to Amber. Crazy.

Harper joins me.

"So, are we in a parallel universe?" I ask. "Because I have no idea who that guy is."

"He *is* pretty drunk," Harper says. She glances down at the floor, then up at me. That shy thing gets me every single time, even when Paige did it and I knew it wasn't real. But Harper . . . it's not a calculated maneuver to get me hot. It's authentic. And still incredibly effective. "Do you, um, want to go for a walk?" she asks.

This could be an invitation to go for a walk or it could be for something more. Either way, I'm in. Even if it means walking to Bonita Springs and back. "Sure."

"We'll be back in a while," I say as Harper puts the pitcher on the table. I reach into the pocket of my jeans and pull out a three-strip of condoms. "Be safe. Have fun. Don't do anything I wouldn't do."

Kevlar looks up at me with a shitty grin. "So that means your mom's a go?"

I smack the back of his head, then thread my fingers through Harper's. "We're outta here."

We cross Estero and cut down one of the beach access lanes, where we leave our flip-flops behind. The sand is cool and damp between my toes as we walk toward the fishing pier and beach shops.

"So what's up with the pocketful of condoms?" she asks. "Did you think you were going to need that many tonight?"

"I bought them for Kevlar. Just in case."

Harper slants a skeptical look my way. "Really?"

"I guarantee the one he carries around in his wallet expired a long time ago," I say. "So I picked some up at the beer store this afternoon because I knew he wouldn't think of it until it was too late."

"That was kind of . . . nice."

I laugh. "Yeah, well, I'm kind of a nice guy."

"Did you keep any for yourself?"

"Nope," I say. "Should I have?"

She shakes her head. "Is that okay?"

I shrug. "I'm not in any rush."

We pass through Times Square, stopping to watch a magician performing for a handful of German tourists. After we buy twist cones at the Dairy Queen, we head back up Estero until we reach her street. "Do you want me to walk you home?"

"I don't want to go home."

"Harper—" I start to tell her that she should face what's bothering her, but what business do I have telling her what to do when I have no idea how to face what's bothering me? "Okay."

"It's just—if we get down there and her car is still in the driveway . . ." Harper trails off. "I don't have a problem with

Alison, but a little warning would have been nice, you know?"

I nod. "That's what I told your dad."

"You did?" Her face and voice go soft, and she kisses me right there on the street corner. Until a passing car honks and someone shouts that we should get a room.

"Do you want to go back to the hotel?" I ask.

"What if the room is . . . occupied?"

I shudder at the mental picture of Kevlar and Amber, and Harper grimaces as if she's imagined the same thing.

"Yeah, never mind," I say. "Let's go to my house."

* * *

The sun is bright through the slats of the blinds when I open my eyes the next morning. The clock on the bedside table says I've slept later than I can remember sleeping since before I went to boot camp. And I feel good. Rested. Like I've—

I've slept all night.

No insomnia. No nightmares. No pills.

No Charlie.

"Hey." Harper's voice is husky with sleep beside me, her arm across my chest. Paige never spent the whole night—she always snuck out before my mom woke up—and I've never brought anyone else here.

Last night I did things with Harper that I leapfrogged

when I was fourteen and having sex with Paige in the horse barn behind her house. It's not that I regret it. I don't. It's just—being with Harper is like getting a do-over.

"Hey back," I say. "You give good sleep."

"Is that what the boys have been saying about me all these years?"

"Yeah, I read it above the urinal in the locker room."

She yawn-laughs. "What time is it?"

I pick up my cell phone. "Almost ten."

"Oh, no!" Harper scrambles out of my bed and re-knots her hair. "I'm going to be late for work."

My mom is in the kitchen when we go downstairs. Her eyebrows shoot up when she sees Harper, then she pins me with a death ray stare loaded with silent scolding. *Travis Henry Stephenson, you better not have been doing what I think you were doing. Not with a sweet girl like Harper Gray.*

"Harper," she says. "What a surprise."

"Yeah, um—nice to see you, Mrs. Stephenson." Harper's face is pink with embarrassment, even though she's got nothing to be embarrassed about.

"Long story," I say. "We've gotta go."

I drop Harper off at the Waffle House and meet up with Kevlar and Moss at the beach. Moss is asleep on a lounge chair, but Kevlar is propped up with a beer in his hand. I'd laugh at his Afghani-tan—tanned face and neck, white everywhere else—but I have one, too. Charlie was the one who dubbed it the Afghani-tan.

"You missed one helluva night, Solo," he says. "We went to this strip club called Fantasy's. Did you know Amber is an exotic dancer?"

It doesn't surprise me. Taking off her clothes for money is within her skill set. I peel off my T-shirt and fish a beer from the depths of the icy cooler. "Dude, she's a *stripper.*"

"Don't be a hater just because your girlfriend is a goddess," Kevlar says. "Amber is a very amenable girl, if you get what I'm sayin'."

"What you're saying is you probably paid sixty bucks for three lap dances, then came back to the hotel alone to liquidate the inventory."

"Fuck you."

"Did you or did you not close the deal, Kenneth?"

"I don't think I want to tell you now." He crosses his arms over his scrawny freckled chest, all huffy, and turns his nose up, pretending to ignore me.

"Kevlar, man, I thought we were BFFs," I say. Moss doesn't open his eyes, but a chuckle rumbles out. "I still have my half of the necklace, and last night I wrote in my diary, 'Dear Diary, Kenneth is my BFF. I hope he gets laid, because it's a special night when a man loses his virginity and contracts a sexually transmitted disease at the same time.'"

"Hey! I used a condom." A shit-eating grin breaks out on his face and I know he wants to rattle off every detail, but just . . . no. I don't need *those* nightmares, too.

"Aw, Moss, our little boy is all grown up." I shake my can. "We should celebrate."

"Solo." Kevlar jumps off his chair. "No."

He runs down the beach and I chase, but he's not faster than I am. I catch him, put him in a headlock, and spray beer in his face. "Congratulations, dude. It's about damn time."

We hang out on the beach for a couple of hours, until my friends have to head back to North Carolina. I sit in the room with them while they're packing.

"Wish I was going back, too," I say.

"Had all the family you can stand?" Moss asks.

They don't know that Peralta "suggested" my extra leave. Or that Charlie, the only person I could talk to about any of this, is part of the reason I'm here. "Yep."

"I love my mother," he says. "But after about four days I had all the mothering I can take."

"Don't cry, Solo." Kevlar comes out of the bathroom carrying all the little soaps and shampoo bottles. "We'll see you next weekend."

"What's next weekend?"

"Kevlar, man, you didn't tell him?" Moss smacks Kevlar in the back of the head, then rummages through his bag. He pulls out a cream-colored envelope and hands it to me. "We all got them. If you had your mail forwarded, you'll probably be getting it any day."

Inside is a matching cream-colored card. An invitation.

In memoriam
LCpl. Charles Thompson Sweeney

The honor of your presence
is requested at a memorial service
Saturday, the fourteenth of August
at five o'clock in the evening
The White Room
1 King Street
St. Augustine, Florida

My mouth goes dry and when I swallow it feels like I have sandpaper caught in my throat. I really don't want to go to a memorial service, but I promised Charlie I'd visit his mom and I haven't done it yet. How do you tell your best friend's mother that everything you could do wasn't enough?

"This Marine is looking forward to pulling out the blues," Kevlar says. "And watching the panties drop."

Moss smacks him upside the head again. "Have some respect. It's a memorial service."

"Dude, if he were alive, Charlie would be the first person to exploit the situation to get laid," Kevlar says. "He'd be all *Wedding Crashers*, Marine style."

It's a fair point. Charlie used to joke about how he was going to buy himself a Purple Heart on eBay so he could use it to get sympathy sex.

"I guess I'll see you guys next weekend, then."

They leave me standing in the hotel parking lot and I'm tempted to go inside to the bar and get wrecked, because the only other place I have to go is home.

* * *

My envelope is lying on the kitchen island when I get there. I tear through the expensive paper, even though I already know what it says, and a folded note falls out with the invitation. It's from Charlie's mom.

Dear Travis,

I hope you will be willing to say a few words at Charlie's memorial service. While I was blessed to have him in my life the longest, you knew him best. He called you brother. He called you friend. I know this is asking a lot and I will understand if you would rather not, but please call me when you decide.

Always,
Ellen Sweeney

"Please don't tell her, Solo." Charlie stands next to me at the island. "She thinks I'm a hero. Don't take that away from her."

"I won't." I rub the heels of my hands against my eyes to make him go away, but he's still there. "But you need to go away."

When I open my eyes, my mom is watching me from the doorway. "Who needs to go away, Travis?"

"No one," I say. "It's nothing. Headache." Lie. I'm not telling my mom my dead best friend was talking to me. Or that I was talking back. "Seriously. It's all good."

I'm not sure she believes me, but she takes a whole key lime pie—my favorite—from the fridge and cuts it into wedges. "I was a little surprised to see Harper Gray coming down my stairs this morning. I hope you're not—"

"I'm not." It doesn't matter how that sentence ends. "She's really . . ." I shrug. "I like her."

It's a crumb, really, but Mom brightens as if I handed her a whole loaf. She slides me a small plate with a sliver of pie on it. "I always knew you could do so much better than Paige Manning."

Laughing, I cut my fork into the dessert. "Yeah, well, I don't know if you're aware of this, but she moved on to Ryan."

"What? No!"

"I'm surprised Dad didn't tell you," I say. "They hooked up while I was gone."

She sighs. "I try to be charitable, but I'm sorry. I really dislike that girl."

"I kinda got that impression."

Mom gets a resigned look on her face. "Well, I guess if she has to . . . *hook up* with one of my boys, I'd rather it be Ryan."

My eyebrows hitch up. "Oh?"

"I know a mother is not supposed to play favorites, and I love you both, but I've always liked you better." She swipes her finger through the whipped cream on the top of her pie.

At first this surprises me. For all the times she stood by while Dad got on my case about one thing or another, I'd never have guessed I was her favorite. "Even though I'm a disappointment?"

"You're not a disappointment, Travis," she says. "You took everything your dad heaped on you and never complained about it." Tears build up in her eyes. "I could see how much you hated it, but it seemed so important to him that I didn't interfere. I'm sorry."

I shrug. "It's okay."

"I went to see you play soccer once," she says. After I quit the football team, I started playing Sunday soccer with the Mexicans out on Kelly Road. It was so much fun to just run up and down a field and not have someone yelling that I was doing it wrong. No game analysis afterward, either. We'd sit on the hood of someone's car and flirt with the girls. "It was so nice to see you happ—"

"Why'd you take him back?"

She presses her fingertips against the stray bits of graham cracker crust dusting the countertop, then brushes them onto my empty plate. "You'll be going back to North Carolina soon and Ryan leaves for Pennsylvania at the end of the month," she says. "I just—I guess I'm afraid of being alone."

"And being with the guy who cheated on you is better? Jesus Christ, Mom, stop being such a doormat."

For a moment she only stares at me. Over the years I've ignored her when she was nagging at me, but I've never been outright disrespectful—even when she pissed me off. "This is not Afghanistan, Travis." Her voice wavers and I can tell I've hurt her. I feel bad about it, but she needs to listen. "Maybe you can speak to your friends that way, but here—"

"This isn't about my choice of words," I say. "I know my going to Afghanistan was hard on you and I'm really, really sorry about that, but that's no excuse for him to step out on you, Mom. I feel like it's my fault when—"

"It's not your fault."

"I know it's not," I say. "But it's not your fault, either."

She picks up the envelope from the memorial service invitation and presses the back flap closed, even though the adhesive is long gone. "I don't know, Travis. When I look back, maybe I neglected him and Ryan—"

"By sending me care packages and getting support from other Marine moms?" I ask. "Seems to me that Dad and Ryan were the ones who should have been supporting you."

"But—"

"No." I push the plate away. "There are no buts. I'm done. If you want to keep pretending he's a stand-up guy, be my guest. But don't expect me to do the same."

"Travis—"

Ignoring her, I head upstairs to my room. On the way, I call Harper.

"What are you doing this weekend?" I ask, closing the door to my room.

"Working."

"Do you think you can get out of it?" My laptop makes a chiming sound as I power it up. What am I going to say about Charlie at the service?

"Possibly. Why?"

"There's a memorial for Charlie up in St. Augustine," I say. "Will you go with me?"

"I'll have to ask my dad," Harper says. "I'm not sure how he'd feel about—"

"Tell him you'll have your own room. On a different floor than mine if that makes him feel any better. Whatever he wants, Harper. Whatever you want. Just go with me? Please?"

I've never begged a girl for anything in my life, but nothing about this memorial is going to be easy. With Harper there . . . I don't know. Maybe it won't be so bad.

"Let me make some calls to cover my shifts," she says. "If I can make it work, I'll go."

Next I dial Charlie's mom. "Ms. Sweeney, this is Travis Stephenson."

"Oh, Travis." She sighs. "I was hoping to hear from you."

"Yes, ma'am, um—I just wanted to tell you I'll be at the

memorial and I can talk about Charlie if, you know, you want."

"That would mean so much to Jenny and me." Her voice catches in her throat and it hits me that as terrible as Charlie's death was for me, it has to be a million times worse for her. "Do you need a place to stay? You're welcome to stay with us."

"No, thank you, ma'am." I lie, "I've already booked a room."

She sniffles back tears. "I'm so looking forward to meeting you, Travis."

"I, um—thank you."

"We'll see you Saturday."

I disconnect the call and look at the blank computer screen, wishing the words would write themselves.

Charlie Sweeney was

Chapter 11

Hours later the cursor still taunts me from the end of those same three words and I'm no closer to finding the ones that come next. I give up trying and flop down on the bed. My eyes are closed when the door creaks open, but I don't open them to see who it is. I already know. "Go away."

"What?" a female voice says. "You're not talking to me now?"

Shit. I am not in the mood to deal with Paige.

The bed sags a little as she sits down on the edge and her fingers touch the button on my shorts. I can feel my body responding to her—just like it always does—but my brain isn't playing along. Even though Harper isn't officially my girlfriend, if she knew about this, she'd be hurt. Or mad.

Probably both. And for the first time in my life, I care about that. My fingers close around Paige's wrist, stopping her. *"Don't."*

She laughs at me in her typical condescending way. "What is it about Harper Gray that's got you so twisted?"

"Why do you care? You dumped me for Ryan."

"I'm not jealous."

"Nobody said you were," I say. "Yet you keep showing up in my room in the middle of the night when your boyfriend is down the hall."

"You can be so stupid sometimes, Travis," she says. "You were supposed to try to get back together with me. You always do."

She sniffles and I look up. She's crying. Not outright bawling or anything, only a tear trickling down her cheek, which is something I've never seen before. She blows out a breath. "Except you went straight for Harper, just like you did back in middle school."

I'm so confused. "So, wait—"

"No." Paige wipes her eyes on the bottom of her tank top. "Shut up. I know the only good thing we've ever had is the sex. I guess one time I wished you'd want me the way you want her."

Sometimes girls make no sense at all. "What are you talking about?"

"I came over last night," she says. "You were sleeping

with her, and all your clothes were on, and—you love her."

"I don't—do you, um—" I stumble over my words. "You don't love me, do you?"

She laughs. "Jesus, you really are an idiot. No, I don't love you. But it would have been nice if you loved me."

"You mean the way Ryan does?"

She stops laughing, because she knows I'm right. My brother is crazy about her in a way I never was. Never will be. Paige has had a string of lovesick schmucks who fell for her and didn't realize she'd never love them back. Even though Ryan and I don't get along all that well, he's still my brother. I don't like the idea of him ending up one of those lovesick schmucks. "He's a lot better for you than I am."

"I know."

I hear the hesitation in her voice. "But?"

"He's not you."

"Well, no shit," I say, which makes her sniffle-laugh. "But if you're not into Rye, don't toy with him. Cut him loose."

She shoulder-bumps me. "If things don't work out between you and Harper—"

"Get out of here." I laugh. "I've got things to do."

Paige leans over and kisses my cheek. "See ya, Trav."

She pulls open my bedroom door and Ryan is standing in the hallway. Of course. The one time that absolutely nothing happens between me and Paige, we get busted. Ryan's face goes to rage instantly. "What the—?"

He rushes me, slamming his hands into the middle of my chest, and pushes me back against the wall. I hear some of the photos tear away from the wall and the head of a thumbtack presses into my back. It happens so fast and I'm still trying to process the fact that Ryan got the drop on me when his fist connects with my eye. The same one Harper hit.

"Ryan, stop it!" Paige grabs his arms and tries to pull him away, but he shakes her off and cocks his fist back to hit me again. I shove him, but the stupid fool comes at me again. One hit? Fine. I deserved that. But I'm not going to be his personal punching bag. Not when he started this. Lowering my shoulder, I hit him in the chest. He grabs on to me and we hit the floor. His fists are pummeling me wherever he can reach, but I've got him pinned to the ground.

"Let him go." Dad grabs the back of my T-shirt, pulling it until I can feel the collar pressing tightly against the front of my neck like a noose. Ryan gets in one last hit, smacking the side of my head with his fist. "What the hell is going on here?"

"Nothing." I reach out to help Ryan up, but he slaps my hand away. "Just a misunderstanding."

"I want you out of here," Dad says, pointing at me.

"Dean—"

"No, Linda." He cuts her off and helps Ryan to his feet.

"Ever since he's come home, Travis has stirred up trouble—
getting you drunk, trying to break up our marriage, and
this isn't the first time he's had Paige over in the middle
of the night. I've had enough."

They're standing in a clump on the other side of my room.
Them versus me. Except Paige, who looks as if she wishes
she were anywhere but here, and Mom is gnawing her lip.
Dad's arm is across my brother's chest, holding Ryan back.

"Well, we finally agree on something." I grab my seabag
and shove in a handful of shirts from the top drawer of my
dresser. "I'm done."

"Travis, wait." My mom steps forward. Out from Dad's
shadow. "You don't have to leave. This is my house—"

"*Your* house?" Dad interrupts.

"It will be mine in the divorce if you don't stop talking," Mom snaps. His eyes go wide, because she never talks
like that, but he stops talking. "Travis isn't the bad guy here,
Dean. He spent his childhood trying to live up to your
impossible expectations and when he decided he didn't want
to do that anymore, *you* were the one who treated him as if
he's worthless. And you've made me feel like I'm wrong for
supporting our son when he was in the middle of a *war*. You
are the bad guy, Dean. You. And *I* have had enough."

I have to do a mental check to make sure my mouth isn't
hanging open because . . . damn, Mom.

"So Travis isn't leaving unless he wants to leave, and things
are going to change around here," she says. "If you want to

stay married to me, you're going to have to straighten up, and if you don't, you need to pack your things and get out."

Dad looks bewildered—like he can't figure out what just happened—but I have no sympathy. Not when I'm so proud of my mom.

"Now," she says. "I'm going back to bed. Paige, you'd be wise to leave now, and Dean—well, what you do is up to you. Good night."

She walks out with some serious dignity, leaving the rest of us standing there in silence. Dad's expression is murderous as he clings to his pathetic insistence that this is my fault. His fists bunch at his sides and his jaw twitches, as if he's considering taking a swing. I meet his glare. "I wouldn't."

He stalks out of the room, his footsteps fading down the stairs, instead of down the hall toward Mom, the way they should. Coward.

"Listen, Rye—" I say.

"Go to hell."

Paige doesn't say anything. She drops the spare key on the end of my bed and leaves. Pain flashes across my brother's face—he won't get the courtesy of a Dear John letter to make the breakup official—before it hardens back to anger.

"Why did you do it?" He won't look at me.

"Do *what*?"

"Sleep with my girlfriend."

"Why did *you* sleep with *my* girlfriend?"

"You get everything, Travis," he says.

"What exactly do I have that you haven't taken, Ryan?" I ask. "You hang out with my friends, drive my car, and steal my girlfriend while I'm in Afghanistan. What more do you want from me? I have nightmares that keep me up at night. You're fucking welcome to those."

Ryan doesn't say anything for a moment. He just looks at the floor. But when he looks up at me, his face is still hard. "I can take one more thing," he says. "You tell Harper or I will."

Shit.

When he's gone and I'm alone, I return to my laptop and the words are still there waiting. Cursor blinking.

Charlie Sweeney was

There's no way I'm going to think of anything tonight. Not with Ryan's threat hanging over me. I close the laptop and get into bed.

* * *

I'm walking down a road in Marjah as the muezzin sings the haunting call, summoning the faithful to prayer. A mud-colored dog lifts its head to watch as our patrol passes by. First me, then Charlie and Moss. Peralta is behind them. The hair on the back of my neck sets me on alert. Something isn't right. But when I try to call out to my friends, my voice won't come. My hands won't lift to flag them down. My feet feel as if they are rooted to the ground. Charlie takes a step forward, his foot landing on the pressure plate of a bomb, and the explosion rattles my teeth, my bones. A cloud of dust envelops him. Shrapnel from the bomb, hidden in the base of a tree, riddles his body and he falls. Movement comes rushing back to my limbs, but when I reach him the world tilts. I'm the one on the ground, not Charlie. I'm the one sprayed with shrapnel that sends searing pain through me. Above me is an Afghan boy. One I've seen before in the streets, begging for whatever we have to offer. He smiles at me as I die.

* * *

My blood is rushing in my ears as I lie in the dark with *only a dream, only a dream, only a dream* repeating in my mind like a mantra. The words don't help. They can't blot out the nightmare. I reach for the bottle of pills on the nightstand and after I take two, I call Harper.

"Travis?" Her voice is gravelly with sleep.

"I forgot it's the middle of the night."

"Shouldn't you be sleeping?"

"I had a nightmare, so I'm awake," I say. "I just took my prescription."

"Do you want me to stay on the phone until you get sleepy?"

"Do you mind?"

She's quiet for a beat and I wonder if she's mentally calculating the hours between now and the time she has to get up for work. I almost hang up so she can go back to sleep, but then she says, her voice soft and low, "I don't mind."

Harper talks for a while. About the sea turtles. About how she's ready to go to college, but that she'll miss her dad when she's gone. About the crab trap they keep in the canal behind their house.

"Depending on the season, we'll get blues or stone crabs," she says. "Usually we'll boil them and freeze the meat until we have enough for crab cakes. Or sometimes we'll make crab dip or alfredo pasta."

"I like crab." I'm starting to get tired and it's making me talk like a three-year-old.

"Me, too," she says. "It's my favorite. Maybe, um— maybe I'll make you crab cakes sometime."

"Okay." A yawn overtakes me.

"Travis?" she says.

"What?"

"Sweet dreams."

"I hope so," I say. "I'm really tired of the bad ones."

"Talk to you tomorrow?"

"Okay." I feel the sleep wave approaching. The one where your words will wash away if you don't say them. "I'm really sorry."

She probably thinks I'm apologizing for waking her up, but before I can tell her that it's for what happened with Paige, she whispers good night and hangs up. At least I think she does. I'm not sure because I'm asleep.

Chapter 12

The sun has barely broken the horizon a few days later, when I pull the Jeep into the driveway at Harper's house. She's waiting on the front porch swing with a yellow duffel bag beside her.

"Hey, you," she calls over the rumble of the engine as she throws the duffel in the back and swings up into the passenger's seat. I catch a whiff of sunscreen as she leans over to drop a kiss on my cheek.

"Hey back," I say. "Thanks for coming with me."

"Sure."

"I can't promise it's going to be a good time."

"That's okay." I can't see her eyes behind her sunglasses, but she's smiling as she twists her hair up into a knot. She makes messy look so damn good. "I've never been to St. Augustine. Have you?"

"Nope."

She's happy and I don't want to spoil it by telling her about Paige. She's going to be pissed. Now would be the perfect time, so she still has a chance to get out of the Jeep and leave me. But I don't want that to happen, so I throw it in reverse, spitting gravel as I back out into the street.

"I brought music." Harper reaches back to her duffel and pulls out her iPod. "What do you want to hear?"

"You pick."

She plugs her iPod into the stereo with one of those fake cassettes and dials up a reggae-sounding band I've never heard before. Harper sings along, her bare feet propped on the dashboard, and I wish I could run off somewhere with her, away from Paige and Charlie and the United States Marine Corps.

I pull in for gas at the Racetrac just before the interstate.

"I'm going in for a Coke," Harper says as I'm punching the buttons on the self-serve pump. "You want one?"

"Yeah, sure."

I'm leaning against the side of the Jeep, waiting for the tank to fill, when she comes out. "I've got something for you," she says.

From behind her back, she dangles a bag of Skittles in front of my face, and it knocks me out that not only does she remember my favorite candy, but buys it for me. Paige never did anything like that. With one hand I snatch the bag. With the other, I wrap my arm around her waist and pull her against me—and kiss her.

The latch on the gas nozzle pops when the tank is full and the pump shuts off, but we don't stop until a voice comes through the little speaker on the pump, asking if I've finished fueling my vehicle.

"Wow," Harper breathes. Her hands are beneath my T-shirt, splayed out on my back, so I'm pretty confident she was as into it as I was. "I should buy you Skittles more often."

"You don't have to buy my love," I say. "I'll kiss you for free anytime you want."

As soon as the words leave my mouth I wish I could spool them back in. *Buy my love?* Jesus, she probably thinks I'm an idiot. Because I *am* an idiot. But she doesn't look freaked out that I dropped the L-word on her. She smiles.

"I already knew that about you, Travis." She gets back in the Jeep. "I read it on the wall in the girls' locker room."

"That," I say with a laugh, "doesn't surprise me at all."

It's pretty much impossible to talk when you're doing eighty with the top down on the interstate, so for the next few hours Harper keeps the music on shuffle and we sing along. I don't claim to be a good singer, but back in high school, Eddie and I got it into our heads that we were going to start a band with him on bass, me on guitar/vocals, and whoever we could find on drums. It was a punk band, so we figured I wouldn't have to sing well.

We drive into the middle of Florida, through towns I've never heard of—past farms and orange groves and trees that aren't palms—until we reach the outskirts of Disney World. The crops there are restaurants, hotels, and tourist attractions, and traffic picks up, because even in the summer there is no escaping the Mouse. Once we're on the other side, the landscape changes again and the green highway signs tell us we're getting close to the beaches. New Smyrna. Daytona. Ormond.

The miles close in on St. Augustine and I start thinking about Charlie. I asked him once, when we were picking through our MREs for the best parts, why he joined the Marines.

"It was the commercial that got me, man," he said, shoveling a plastic forkful of sloppy joe into his face. "You know the one where the guy jumps into the pool and comes up out of the water in full gear?"

I had no idea what he was taking about. I never paid attention to the recruiting ads on TV and I hadn't even considered enlisting until the day I walked into the recruiter's office. I had no idea that most guys don't sign up and ship to boot camp a few weeks later, the way I did.

"My mom's a hippie type," Charlie said. "She was always talking about how I should take a gap year between high school and college to *find myself.* I think she was expecting me to backpack my way across Europe or live in a Buddhist monastery in Thailand. So I'm watching TV one day and that commercial comes on and I start thinking about how fuck-ing cool it would be to be a Marine."

Moss, who was sitting with us while we ate, just shook his head and muttered, "Boot."

Charlie laughed, because insults never stuck to him. He was rubber that way. The only thing that would have ever gotten under his skin was if the other guys had made fun of his mom being a lesbian, but I was the only one who knew. "So I go to her and I'm like, 'Mom, I'm going to join the Marines.' She's *completely* horrified on account of her being a tree-hugging peace freak, but she says, 'Well, if that's what you really want—but, Charlie, wouldn't you rather go on a vision quest or something? I know a guy in New Mexico. He has peyote.'" He laughed again, his mouth full of food. "My mom—the only parent on the planet to try and talk her kid *into* doing drugs to keep him *out* of the Marines."

It's just past lunchtime when we roll into St. Augustine on Highway 1. My face feels tight from the wind and sun, and the end of Harper's nose is a little bit pink. My insides are bunched up now that we're here, even though the memo-rial service isn't until later this evening, and I still haven't figure out what—if anything—to tell Harper.

"You hungry?" I ask as she lowers the volume from highway to city.

"Definitely."

"How do you feel about barbecue?" On the side of the street is a little soul food place. The smell of barbecued meat hangs in the air and my stomach growls out loud.

"I think your stomach already decided," she says. "But that sounds good."

We go inside and order ribs, greens, and macaroni and cheese off a menu board spelled out in mismatched letters.

"Do you want to sit in or out?" I ask.

"In," Harper says as we sit down at a picnic table. "The air-conditioning feels good."

She's right, it is, but shit—I have to take off my sunglasses. Because it would be weird if I didn't. And as soon as I do, she notices the black eye.

"What happened to your eye?"

"I got in a fight with Ryan."

"Over Paige?"

"Why would you think that?"

She picks up a rib. "Because if you were going to get in a fight with your brother, chances are it would be over a family thing or Paige. I went with logic."

"I, um—I kind of hooked up with her since I've been back."

She puts down the rib and starts gathering all of her food onto the tray we brought from the counter. She does it really fast. Angry fast.

"Harper, I didn't mean—"

"Don't talk." Her voice is low and controlled as she

stands with the tray. Quiet, so she doesn't draw attention. "Or I'll dump my lunch on you and that would be a waste of good food. I'm going to the Jeep."

I get up, but she cuts me with a look so sharp it drops me back down on the bench. My stomach growls again, reminding me I'm hungry, but to dig into my lunch would be a dick move. On top of all the others I've made since I've known her, I mean. From the window I can see her sitting in the passenger seat with the tray on her lap. She doesn't look my direction at all. So I eat.

And try to think of a way to fix things. Again.

She's still in the Jeep when I go outside, but the tray is gone, and she goes out of her way to not look at me. I check the computer-printed directions to the hotel and then start the engine.

"Why?" Harper says as I pull out into traffic. At first I think she's asking me why I slept with Paige, but then she continues. "Why would you bring me all the way to St. Augustine and then tell me you hooked up with your ex-girlfriend?"

"If I told you at home, you wouldn't come."

"You're a shithead, Travis," she says. "And I'm stupid for thinking you could possibly feel the same way about me as I do about you."

"I do."

"No, you don't. Because I would never do that to you."

Just like that I'm leveled. Ripped open. She could have

shot me and it would be less painful. I know. I've been shot. Only I lived.

"Harper, I'm sorry," I say.

She doesn't reply, but I guess I'm not really expecting an answer. I've done a lot of apologizing and can see how that might call my sincerity into question—and piss her off.

We reach downtown and it sucks she's not speaking to me, because St. Augustine is cool. The buildings are old and historic, some dating back to the 1700s, and the Spanish moss dripping from the oak trees in the park make it feel like we're somewhere other than Florida. I wonder if Harper likes it as much as I do, but I don't ask. Instead I ask her if she wants me to drive her back to Fort Myers.

"And prove to my dad that you're as big an idiot as you were in seventh grade?" She snorts. "I don't think so. Let's just go to the hotel. Then you can do your thing and I can do mine until the service."

Shit.

"I don't want—"

"It doesn't matter what you want," she says. "What I want right now is for you to leave me alone."

"But—" I want to explain. Tell her that what happened with Paige didn't mean anything.

"Just don't," she says. "Because if you try to tell me that it didn't *mean* anything or it *just happened* or that we weren't *technically* together when you hooked up with Paige, I will punch you in the face again."

And that's the thing. There isn't any good reason why I slept with Paige. I didn't do it to get revenge on Ryan or because I wanted her back. I just did it because I could. And there's really no excuse for that.

We don't talk again until we reach the hotel, which is probably the fanciest place I've ever seen. The lobby is filled with overstuffed leather chairs, Spanish tapestries, golden chandeliers, and a tiled fountain. I feel like a peasant in the palace as I approach the black-vested man behind the marble-topped reception desk. He lifts his eyebrows when I tell him I have a reservation—as if he can't believe it either—and for a moment I'm annoyed.

"Name?" he asks.

"Stephenson."

His fingers click on his computer keyboard. "Two rooms," he reads off the screen. "One night."

"I want to pay for my own room," Harper says.

"Harper . . ." All the while I was in Afghanistan, my pay was direct deposited into my bank account. Since I've spent very little money over the past year, I can afford these rooms. They're expensive. Too much for what amounts to a couple of well-decorated bedrooms, but I wanted to impress her. Now I just want to make it up to her. "I've got it."

She doesn't say anything, but she walks as far away from me as she can as the bellman carries our luggage to the fourth floor. It's strange letting someone else carry my sea-bag. Also, my dusty bag looks so alien in a hotel that looks like a Spanish castle. We stop first at Harper's room. Although she doesn't say anything as she goes inside, she glances back at me before closing the door.

My room is beside hers, with a big iron bed covered with soft-looking bedding and a wrought iron balcony overlooking downtown and Matanzas Bay. I tip the bellman for the bags, hang my uniform in the wardrobe, and then go out onto the balcony. On the street below, a horse-drawn carriage filled with tourists rolls past, the horses' hooves clip-clopping on the pavement. Harper comes outside and awkwardness fills the small space between her balcony and mine. There's no reason we can't both be out here, but it feels weird. I want to ask her to go driving around St. Augustine with me. Or to the beach. Or even to go to that stupid wax museum down the street to look at fake Michael Jackson and fake Michael Jordan. Before I can do any of that, she goes back inside.

Chapter 13

It's nearly five o'clock when I knock on the door to Harper's room. I've never worn my blue dress uniform before, so it's starch-stiff and new-smelling, and I'm not sure my medals and qualification badges are positioned according to regulation. Also, the heavy jacket is hot—even in the air-conditioning—and I'm sweating between my fingers in these gloves. This uniform might impress girls, but it's uncomfortable. Especially compared to my cammies, which were sandblasted to a salty faded softness.

I'm tugging down on the hem of my jacket when Harper steps out into the hall, wearing a black dress that somehow manages to be memorial service respectable and sexy at the same time. She's straightened her hair again and her black sandals make her nearly as tall as me.

"Wow, Harper, you look beautiful." I offer her my arm as an older couple walks past and I hope she doesn't blow me off. They glance at each other and smile as she slips her hand under my arm. Her fingers are shaking.

"Thank you." Her voice is quiet, as if she doesn't want to talk to me but also doesn't want to be rude. Which is okay with me. I'll take that. "You, too. I mean, you don't look beautiful. You look really . . . good . . ."

I'm sure I look like an idiot—and this might be the only remotely nice thing she says to me for the rest of the night—but I can't keep the smile off my face. "Thanks."

The banquet room is only a couple blocks from the hotel, so we leave the Jeep in the parking lot and walk down King Avenue. We get a lot of looks. Kevlar is right about the effect the dress blues have on girls.

We've barely entered the banquet room when Charlie's mom appears. Ellen Sweeney looks exactly like her son. If, you know, Charlie were a middle-aged woman with thick black dreadlocks wearing a too-tight, red Chinese-style dress with gold dragons all over it.

"Oh, Travis, you are much more handsome in person than in pictures." She jingles as she reaches up to touch my face—her arm so full of bracelets it seems like she shouldn't even be able to lift it—then pulls me into a hug. "I'm so glad to see you. It's *good* to have you here."

I reach my arms around her, feeling awkward as I hug her back. She smells like a hippie. Like incense or something. It tickles my nose and it's not the most pleasant thing I've ever smelled, but I let her hold on to me as long as she needs. I'm getting used to the hugging. When she pulls away, her eyes are shiny with tears. "Thank you for coming."

"I wouldn't have missed it for anything," I say.

Charlie's mom turns to Harper and squeezes both her hands. "Aren't you adorable?" she says. "I'm Ellen."

"I'm Harper."

"Thank you, Harper, for keeping Travis company on his journey."

Charlie told me once that his mom's personal philosophy is kind of like a salad bar. She picks her favorite parts—a little dogma here, a little karma there—until she's assembled a heaping plate of strange. I probably should have warned Harper, but with her being mad at me, it slipped my mind. But Harper doesn't miss a beat as she smiles at Ellen. "I wish I could have met you under better circumstances," she says. "I'm sorry about Charlie."

Ellen pats her hand and touches her cheek. "If you'll excuse me." As Charlie's mom steps away to greet someone new, she looks back at Harper. "Someone famous—I have forgotten right now just who—once said the heart has its reasons that reason does not know. Food for thought, that."

Harper swings her head in my direction, giving me a narrow-eyed glare. As if I had something do with it.

"Don't look at me." I throw my hands up in surrender. "I just met the woman."

I'm not sure she believes me, though.

Across the room I see Kevlar, Moss, Ski, and Starvin' Marvin. We call him Starvin' Marvin—or usually just Marv—because he's tall and skinny, and with his head shaved he looks like the African kid the boys adopted on *South Park*. I wasn't as tight with Ski and Marv as Charlie, Kevlar, and Moss, but we hung out together night after night in Afghanistan, circled around the fire pit, smoking, telling dirty jokes, and arguing over the hotness of female celebrities. Peralta is with them, too. "Charlie told me she thinks she has, as she puts it, a touch of the ESP," I tell Harper.

"She's . . . unusual," she says. "But I like her."

"Yeah. Me, too."

Harper follows my sight line and spots nearly all of Kilo Company—a forest of dress blues. "I, um—need to use the ladies' room," she says, and leaves me to join my friends alone.

In the corner of the room a band plays a reggae-fied version of one of the sad Beatles songs, and the people dotting the room are dressed in everything from dark business suits to tie-dyed hippie skirts with those jingly ankle bracelets. There's even one woman with bare feet. She's got about half a dozen plastic grocery bags draped over her arm and she looks as if she hasn't showered in a while, so she might be a homeless lady Charlie's mom invited in for a free meal.

"Here's the man." Kevlar whacks me on the back as I walk up. He smells like whiskey. "How's it going, Solo? Did you bring the whip?" He giggles. "Because you're whipped. Get it?"

"That was weak, Kenneth," I say as I shake hands all around. "Get back to me when you've got something original."

"Whatever." He works his tongue into the empty space where his dip would be, making his lower lip stick out. "Where's your girl?"

"Ladies' room," I say. "But she's kind of pissed at me right now."

"What'd you do?" Moss asks.

"I hooked up with my ex."

"The"—Kevlar air-mimes an enormous rack in front of his chest—"that ex?" I might not have carried around a picture of Paige, but that doesn't mean I didn't describe her.

"That's the one," I say.

"How'd she find out?" he asks.

My face goes hot as I admit I told her.

"Solo . . ." Kevlar shakes his head at me. "For a smart guy, you can be such a dumbass."

I don't tell him I didn't have much of a choice.

"Don't listen to him," Moss says. "Messing with your ex when you've got a good thing going is a bonehead move, but telling her the truth is the honorable thing."

"Honorable, my ass." Marv leans forward and pokes me in the chest with his finger with each word. "It's plain and simple stupid. What she don't know don't hurt her. Period."

"So if your girl stepped out on you while we were in Cali last year for training, you wouldn't want to know about it?" Ski is always the devil's advocate in an argument, especially with Marv, who gets worked up easily.

Marv's forehead wrinkles as his eyebrows pull together. "You know something I don't?"

Ski laughs. "It's a hypothetical."

"A hypo-what?"

"A *what-if*, you retard."

"Oh. Well, that's different," Marv says. "I'd want to know if she's been playing me for a fool while I was gone. And I'd beat the crap out of the guy she's been banging."

"So why doesn't Solo's girl deserve to know?"

"Is that how you got the fresh black eye?" Kevlar asks. "Harper punch you again?"

"No, my brother hit me when he caught me with his girl-friend," I admit, which cracks them all up. And it would be funny, if Harper didn't hate me. Thinking about her makes me feel like my insides are nothing but a series of knots, and it makes me not want to be here right now.

"Stephenson, you got a second?" Peralta asks, like he's reading my mind. His voice is quiet. Even when he was pissed at us he rarely raised it. We step away from the others. "You doing okay?"

"Just suffering from a raging case of stupidity."

Even his laugh is quiet. We walk in silence for a few beats. "Are you . . . getting things squared away?" he asks.

"Yeah."

If he knows I'm lying, Peralta doesn't mention it.

"Listen," he says. "I just wanted to let you know that Leonard volunteered you for bomb dog school."

"Me?" I deflate a little. It's not like my plan for doing the recon course was set in stone, but training to be a bomb dog handler isn't something I've ever considered.

"He asked me to recommend someone," Peralta says. "I chose you because I know you'll do a good job . . . and I think it could help you."

"I don't have a choice, do I?"

He smiles and pats me on the shoulder. "Consider yourself voluntold, but trust me on this, okay?"

Harper comes back into the banquet room as Charlie's mom and a small blond woman I'm guessing is Jenny step up to a podium with a microphone. "Welcome, everyone. If you'll all take a seat, we'll begin in a moment."

The undercurrent of conversation ebbs away as everyone finds a chair, the Marines a solid row in front. I leave a seat on the end for Harper. Her thigh touches against mine when she sits and even after she shifts away it feels warm, like it's still there.

"Thank you," Charlie's mom says, reaching out to take the blond woman's hand. "Jenny and I thank you all for coming today and sharing in the celebration of our son's life."

Kevlar turns and makes a did-you-know-about-this? face, but I shrug my shoulder a little in a silent *get over it.*

Ellen talks for a while, taking us back to when Charlie was a little kid and was horrified to find flamingo on the menu at a restaurant—it was really filet mignon. I didn't know that kid, but I envy his life because even though his mom is a little strange, they were connected in a way I've never been with my parents. They did things together. Went places that didn't involve football.

As Charlie's mom talks, I catch a glance at Harper out of the corner of my eye. She's wiping her nose with the back of her hand, so I pull off my gloves and hand her one. I'm probably breaking some stupid USMC uniform regulation, but she doesn't have a tissue and the glove is absorbent enough. Her words hiccup in her throat when she whispers thank you.

Charlie's mom doesn't try to paint him as a patriot whose love of country came before anything else. He was like the rest of us—trying to figure out what he wanted from life and the best way to get it. She's strong, though, standing up there in front of everyone with her eyes all shiny, but not breaking down as she talks about a son she doesn't have anymore.

When she's finished, she looks at me. "Before he died, Charlie would e-mail me as often as he could and his letters were always peppered with Solo this and Travis that. So I'd like to invite Travis Stephenson to say a few words."

I stand up and look into the middle distance, trying to calm nerves that haven't been this jangled since the last firefight before we left Afghanistan. No matter how many times we engaged the Taliban, it was always completely butt-clenching scary. I blow out a breath and though I don't look at her, I think I feel Harper touch my palm. I curl my fingers around the spot, holding it there, then go to the podium. Ellen smiles at me and I wait for her and Jenny to sit down before I begin.

"Many nights in Afghanistan we played poker," I say. "Since none of us carried much cash, we'd use make-believe money. At last tally, I owe Charlie eight million dollars—" Charlie's mom gives a little chuckle from the front row, which sends a ripple of quiet laughter through the room and dissipates my fear that a joke would be in bad taste. I give Ellen a grin. "I *really* hope you're not planning to collect."

Her eyes are full and she puts her fingers over her mouth as she smiles. I stand there for a moment, looking out at the crowded room. It's as if all of St. Augustine turned out for this. Family. High school friends. Ex-girlfriends, maybe. Someone here has to be more qualified to make this speech than I am.

"I, um—I struggled for a long time trying to figure out what I was going to say and now that I'm here, I still have no idea," I say. "The things that keep coming to mind are not really appropriate, like his fondness for Miss November, or the time he put . . . Yeah, never mind about that."

I clear my throat and look for a spot in the back of the room, so I don't have to see tissues and tears. Instead, I see

Charlie. He's leaning against the wall like he's waiting to hear what I'm going to say about him. Like he's waiting for me to tell his truth.

"The thing is, Charlie was just . . . When I first met him, I thought he was a complete motard—ridiculously motivated to be a Marine, you know? Because he'd volunteer for anything, and who does that? But then I realized that's who he was. He attacked life so he wouldn't miss out on anything, and if I can tell you one thing about Charlie that you don't already know it's that he went out of this world as bravely as he made his way through it."

My eyes search out Charlie, but he's gone.

I look at his mom.

"He was the person all of us should be, but most of us aren't. And if I could have taken his place to buy him a little more time in the world, I'd have done it. I'm sorry I couldn't."

Ellen shakes her head and I know she's telling me I don't have to be sorry, but how can I not be? How can it be okay that I'm here and Charlie isn't? I step away from the podium and my empty seat is right there. But when Charlie's mom comes up to introduce Peralta, I quietly excuse myself to her.

And I leave.

Chapter 14

Harper says my name as I leave the room, and even though I'm being disrespectful for walking out in the middle of the memorial service, I don't stop. I can't stop. Because my eyes are watering and I'm afraid I'm about to lose my shit. I walk fast, my shoes making sharp taps on the sidewalk as I head toward the hotel. My hands clench and unclench at my sides. I suck in large lungfuls of air and release long breaths. I need to get away from downtown St. Augustine, where tourists are still roaming the streetlamp-lit sidewalks, blissfully unaware that Charlie Sweeney is dead.

I take a shortcut down a side alley that leads to the back entrance of the hotel. Heading for the pool, I work open the clasp on the collar of my uniform. The pool deck is empty in the fading light and all the lounge chairs are lined up in a straight row with fresh towels folded on the ends. I drop the heavy jacket on one chair and my trousers on another as I strip down to my boxers. Leaving my socks balled up at the edge of the pool, I dive in.

As I churn through the water, my breath and brain work in tandem and I don't have to think. I only count my strokes—*one, two, one, two, one, two*—until the muscles in my shoulders burn and the sadness, the rage, I feel is under control. I have no idea how long I've been in the water or how many lengths I've swum when I stop. The sky has faded from dusk to dark—so I know it's been a long time—and Harper is standing at the edge of the pool, holding a towel.

My arms shaking from the exertion, I haul myself out of the water and stand there on the pool deck, dripping water everywhere. As she wraps the towel around my shoulders, her eyes meet mine. "You okay?"

If I were naked, I'd feel less exposed than I do right now. But I tell her the truth. "No."

Harper doesn't say anything as I dry off and wrap the towel around my waist. She just waits until I'm done, then takes my hand like I'm a little kid. I hope she's leading me somewhere good, because I've had about as much as I can take. My insides feel hollowed out and empty. I'm tired. Of everything.

We're at the entrance to the hotel when I remember my uniform. "I forgot my . . ." I stop and look back, but the lounge chairs are empty. Shit.

"I took care of it."

"Oh." She's only being nice to me because I'm a fucking mess. "Thanks."

We don't talk in the elevator up to our rooms. I just stare at the floor until the bell rings and the doors slide open. Harper never lets go of my hand, but it doesn't feel like other times when I've held her hand. Right now it's a lifeline.

"Did, um—was Charlie's mom upset that I left?" I ask as she slides the keycard into the lock on my door.

"She understands, Travis," Harper says. "I understand."

Even after all that time in the pool, my eyes start watering again. I grind the heels of my hands against them, but this time I can't keep the tears at bay and I hate myself for breaking down.

She closes the door behind us and puts her arms around me. I bury my face against her neck and everything inside of me comes out in ugly, choking sobs that I've never heard before. No matter how rough my dad was on me, or how hard things got in boot camp, or how scared I was in Afghanistan, I never cried. Ever. And I know I should be embarrassed, but this is Harper, who doesn't try to tell me everything is going to be okay. She stands there and keeps me from drowning.

Until it's over and I'm quiet.

If it's possible to feel beyond empty, I feel it. I'm a Travis Stephenson–shaped space that needs to be filled in.

"Are you hungry?" It's a strange moment for Harper to ask that question, but I guess it makes sense. There was a dinner at the memorial service and I missed it. Also, I can't hang on to her forever. Even though I kind of like the idea of that.

"Not really."

She pulls back a little and looks at me. "Why don't you put on some dry clothes? I'll go change and—I don't know. We can watch a movie or talk or whatever."

On any other given day, I'd pin my own assumptions to the word "whatever" and let it get me hot and bothered. At the moment, though, her definition of "whatever" is good enough for me. "Yeah, sure."

While she's gone I pull on a pair of clean shorts, then flop down on the bed and start flipping through the TV channels. My eyelids feel heavy. They slide down like window shades, fly back open once, then close.

* * *

I'm walking down a road in Afghanistan with my fire team. Charlie is out in front, and Moss and Peralta are somewhere behind me. The street is deserted. Even the dogs have scattered. Something is about to go down. The hair on the back of my neck rises and dread slides down my spine.

A bullet smacks into the wall beside me. I'm saved by only five inches of air. I duck into a doorway as another shot cracks through the air and I see Charlie fall on the road.

"Charlie's hit!" I don't know if I'm yelling or if it's someone behind me, but I hear it in my head, so maybe it's me.

Crouching, I run toward my friend, the bullets buzzing past me. Pause. Fire. Run again. Although Charlie isn't more than ten or fifteen meters away, the distance takes forever.

"Charlie. Buddy. Hang on."

I yell for a corpsman and try to stop the bleeding, but it's not stopping. Blood covers my dirt-caked fingers as I try to find the vein and the ground around Charlie's head turns to dark mud.

"Solo." His fingers clutch uselessly at my sleeve.

Another round of AK fire peppers the ground around me, puffing up dust. A bullet grazes my upper arm and it feels like I've been smacked with a baseball bat. Moss moves out in front of us, laying down suppressive fire with the automatic weapon.

"Hang on, Charlie," I repeat. *"You're going to make it. You can do this."*

Except he doesn't make it.

His eyes are blank as they stare up into the Afghan sky and his chest has stopped moving. A bullet zings past and I don't even have time to think about what just happened. I drop to my belly in the bloody dirt, my shoulder burning like fire. My eye to my rifle sight, I see him—the Talib in the black turban with an AK pointed at me.

I line him up. And then I kill him.

* * *

I sit up, awake, with my heart whizzing around in my chest like a bottle rocket, and Harper standing at the foot of my bed. I lift my hands to check for blood, but I know it was a dream. The trouble with this dream, though, is that it's true.

"It was our fault," I say. "Charlie's and mine."

She sits cross-legged on the bed, facing me. Her dress is gone, replaced by her faded red shorts and a Clash T-shirt. Her feet are bare and for the first time I notice that her toenails are painted red.

"We were operating out of an old yellow schoolhouse, and nearly every time we went outside the wire, we were ambushed," I say. "Even when you're expecting an ambush, you never know when or where it's going to go down. So most times we'd be walking along some dirt track some-where, they'd start shooting at us, and we'd end up waist-deep in a muddy canal for the next five or ten minutes, shooting back. They'd run away, we'd chase them, they'd blend into the population, and we'd be left pissed off and wet, with no prospect of a hot shower when we got back."

Harper watches my face and I know she's wondering if I'll lose it again. I won't.

"The day Charlie was killed, though, it was different," I continue. "Charlie and me . . . we saw this little kid with a cell phone. A lot of times local guys would use their phones to tell the Taliban our position. So we saw this kid, but we didn't say anything because he was just a little boy, you know?"

Harper nods, but I don't know if she can understand. He was one of the kids in the crowd when we handed out soccer balls and beanbag dolls just a day earlier. He'd bounce up and down with excitement every time we gave stuff away, like it was the first time anyone had ever given him anything. He once tried to grab a whole handful of pens from me. How could *that* kid be suspicious? Except we should have been suspicious when we saw him with a cell phone. We should have reported him to Peralta.

"A few minutes later, we were ambushed," I say. "Charlie was shot and while I was trying to stop the bleeding, I got hit."

Her eyes widen and move to the fading red scar on my upper arm. Moss bandaged it up before we carried Charlie's body back to the base. The wound wasn't bad enough to send me home or anything, and I went back out on patrol again the next day.

My throat goes dry.

"I couldn't save him," I say. "I failed him twice. And I never told anyone."

The official report says I risked my own life in an attempt to save that of a fellow Marine, sustaining a bullet wound and killing an enemy combatant in the process. It sounds a lot more heroic on paper than it was, though. Especially because when it happened I remember rage, not bravery.

"The thing is . . ." I stop and run my hand across the top of my head, trying to find the right words. "Charlie's dead and I'm still alive, and I don't think I deserve to be."

"Do you think he'd agree?"

"I don't know," I say. "He'd probably tell me to stop being an idiot."

Harper's smile is so gentle and sweet. "Sounds like good advice to me," she says.

I laugh a little. "Knowing it and doing it are two different things. I don't—I don't know if I can."

She crawls up to sit beside me, takes the remote, and presses the button for one of the premium movie channels. "Maybe you should talk to someone," she says. "Someone who can help you, I mean. A professional."

"Yeah, maybe."

The movie is one of those '80s Brat Pack types about a poor girl in love with a rich boy who doesn't know she's alive. Not my type of film, but Harper wriggles her way under my arm and rests her head against my shoulder, and suddenly I couldn't care less what's playing on the television screen.

"Hey, Harper," I say. "About what happened with Paige—"

"Let's not," she says, her eyes fixed on the TV screen. "Just consider it strike two."

"That's pretty forgiving of you."

"Yeah, well, I don't really want to kick you when you're down, but mostly for some crazy reason"—her face tilts up and she gives me this shy little grin—"I think you might be worth it."

I nod. "I totally am."

She laughs and elbows me in the ribs. "So." She settles back to watch the movie. "Do you want to do anything special tomorrow?"

I want to suggest something cheesy and touristy—like the Fountain of Youth or the wax museum—and the words are right there in my mouth, waiting to be spoken. But exhaustion crashes over me before I can let them out. I wake just before sunrise to find myself spooned up behind Harper, her ponytail tickling my nose. Something I'm not ready to name works itself under the grip of Charlie's death and loosens it, and keeps the nightmares at bay when I fall back asleep.

Chapter 15

Harper wakes up and for a moment, before she opens her eyes, I feel—strange. As if last night was a one-night stand and I should bail before we have to speak to each other. Except that makes no sense because we didn't have sex and I fell asleep with my face against the top of her head. I might have even drooled in her hair.

It's just—I'm embarrassed. She's seen a side of me I don't really know. And I guess that could be considered a good thing—because I trust her with it—but it doesn't stop the flash of panic that she's seen too much.

Then her eyes open and she blinks, her face scrunched up with sleepiness, and the weirdness dissolves. After that, she smiles and my brain dissolves.

"Hey." Her voice cracks with the first word of the day.

"Hey back," I say, my voice low beside her ear. She shivers. I love that.

"Have you been awake long?" Harper asks.

"An hour, maybe." My fingers find bare skin where the bottom of her T-shirt has inched up and slide my hand underneath. Her skin is warm from sleep. The tiny catch in her breath makes me grin.

She shifts to kiss me. "Why didn't you wake me?"

"Just didn't." My thumb grazes the underside of her breast—and my cell phone rings. "Shit," I say against her mouth.

Harper laughs. "You should get that."

"Probably," I agree, kissing her as the ringing continues. "But I don't want to."

My mouth still on hers I reach for the phone on the bedside table. She pushes me away so I can answer. "This better be good," I say.

"Well, good morning to you, too." Charlie's mom pretends to be offended, but I can hear the laughter in her voice. "I didn't wake you, did I? I wanted to catch you before you had breakfast so you and Harper could join us at the house."

I look at Harper in my bed, her hair all crazy from sleep, and I do not want to have breakfast with Charlie's mom, but it would be impolite to refuse. "Yes, ma'am, we'll be right over."

As I scribble down the address, Harper doesn't wait for

me to tell her where we're going. She scrambles out of bed and heads for her own room, leaving me with the prospect of yet another cold shower.

* * *

"That's the place, right there." Harper points from her side of the Jeep at a squatty purple house with yellow trim and flower boxes full of red flowers. It should be an antiques shop, or where someone's grandma lives, but a painted sign hanging from the front porch roof and bordered with white Christmas lights says it's the home of Sweet Misery Tattoos. I park along the curb in front of the shop.

Bells jingle on the front door handle as I open it for Harper and we're in a living room that's been converted into a waiting room with an old leather couch, a cash register counter filled with body jewelry, and a coffee table full of tattoo magazines. A wooden curtain with an image of the Buddha on it hides the studios and a rope across a set of stairs bears a sign that says *Family, Friends, & US Marines Only.*

"Travis, is that you?" Charlie's mom's voice drifts down from upstairs, along with the scent of breakfast sausage. "Come on up."

The upper floor is a converted apartment with a small kitchen area, where Jenny is crumbling the sausage over a row of flour tortillas, and a living room loaded with religious paraphernalia. Mexican Guadalupe candles, Buddhas, the Hindu goddess chick with all the arms. There's a velvet Jesus painting hung above the couch. I wonder how she has the time for all those deities—and which one of them claimed Charlie. I imagine him hanging with a big-bellied, laughing Buddha—like the little version he carried in his pocket for luck. It had a worn spot on the side from being rubbed.

Today his mom is channeling her inner pirate with a red-and-white-striped shirt and her dreads tied up in a skeleton-print bandanna. She smothers Harper and me with patchouli-scented hugs that make me sneeze. She's smiling, but I recognize the sadness around the corners of her eyes. "How are you today, Travis?"

"I'm good," I say. "I, um—wanted to apologize for walking out of the service last night. It was rude and I'm sorry."

She takes my face in her hands. "You have nothing to apologize for, my darling. Your path is your own and you had to follow it."

I reach into the pocket of my shorts and pull out Charlie's death letter. When we found out we were assigned to a unit being deployed to a war zone, it was suggested we write last letters home—just in case. We made a deal that if one of us was killed, the other would deliver the letter in person. I don't know what Charlie's letter says. I've been tempted to read it, but I never did. "I also need to give you this." I hand Ellen the letter. "I didn't read it."

She tucks it in her pocket without reading. "Are you hungry?"

I haven't eaten anything since lunch yesterday, so yes, I'm seriously hungry. Concave hungry. "Yes, ma'am."

"Then sit," she says. "I'll make coffee."

Harper and I sit at the scarred wooden table while Ellen brews coffee. She babbles about how she only buys a certain brand of fair trade beans from Ecuador and armchair quarterbacks the way Jenny assembles the breakfast burritos, all the while some crazy Sufi pan flute music—which Ellen claims is supposed to be soothing—warbles in the background. They're laughing and joking, and although Charlie is gone, they're happy in a way my family can never seem to manage. We've never had a meal like this, unless you count the time Mom and I ate Harper's shrimp recipe at the kitchen island with Aretha Franklin singing about a chain of fools. I can see why Charlie was so close to his mom.

"Hey, um—I'll be right back," I tell Harper, my chair scraping on the wood floor as I push away from the table.

I go back down the stairs to the empty tattoo shop and dial my mom's number on my cell phone.

"Travis." My name comes out like she's been holding her breath. "How are you?"

For so long I've lied to her, either to keep from having to talk to her or to keep from having to tell her the truth. "I guess I'm doing okay," I say. "This thing with Charlie has been pretty tough and, I don't know—I think I need to talk to someone. I need help."

"Would you like me to set up an appointment for you?"

"Yes. Please."

"I can set you up with my therapist," she says.

I don't know what to say to this. My mom is seeing a therapist? I run my hand over my head. "Hey, um, Mom, I've gotta go because we're having breakfast with Charlie's mom, but I wanted to tell you—" I don't remember the last time I said the words. "I, um—"

The line is silent for a moment as my mom waits for the words, but then she finishes it for me. "I love you, too, Travis."

When I get back upstairs, breakfast is on the table and Harper is telling Jenny and Ellen about her plans for college. "I'm starting second semester, so I can save up a little more money," Harper says. "I qualify for financial aid, but I want to have some extra cash and maybe buy a car."

I always thought that her dad probably did okay as the host of a morning radio show—they're local celebrities—so I'm surprised that she needs financial aid.

"My dad and his on-air partner, Joe, offered to take a syndication deal so I'd have the money for tuition," Harper says, reading my mind. "And, God, you have no idea how badly I wanted to say yes, but I'd hate myself if they did it just so I don't have to pay back college loans, you know? My dad put himself through college, so I guess I can do it, too."

Charlie's mom claps. "I applaud your industry, Harper, and for taking responsibility for your future."

Harper blushes. "I, um—thanks."

After breakfast, Jenny asks Harper to help her with the dishes, while Ellen asks me to go to the shop with her. "I want to show you something," she says as I follow her down the stairs and through the bamboo Buddha curtain. She strips off her shirt, revealing a plain gray sports bra, and turns around so her back is to me. On her upper back, near her shoulder, is a Celtic cross with Charlie's name woven into the knot design. Inked beneath are his birth and death dates.

Not knowing what else to say, I tell her it's cool. I mean, it is cool—for a tattoo.

"I designed it myself." She tugs her shirt back on. "I still have the stencil if you'd like one."

Most of the Marines I know have tattoos. Ski has a massive back piece of a Marine field cross and the names of his friends who died in Iraq. Kevlar went out right after boot camp to get the *Death Before Dishonor* tattoo. Even Moss has a meat tag. It's the inked equivalent of a dog tag so in case a Marine gets his legs blown off by a roadside bomb—because we keep one dog tag in our boot—his body can still be identified. I've never wanted a tattoo, but Ellen's face wears a hopefulness that makes it impossible to refuse. "Yeah, sure."

"Take off your shirt and sit."

I do as she says and watch while she prepares, filling tiny plastic cups with ink and putting new needles in her tattoo machine. "Music?" she asks.

"Anything but that Sufi crap."

She smiles and presses a remote control. The Clash spills through the speakers. Nice.

"Charlie used to say that, too. He'd say, 'Mom, why can't you listen to normal embarrassing music like Celine Dion or Journey or something?'" She drops her voice and she almost sounds like him. It makes me laugh. She rolls her stool up behind me. "I don't know if this will hurt, but I suspect your pain threshold is high enough that it won't."

"Okay."

The tattoo machine begins to buzz and when she touches it against my skin, the sensation is like someone pulling my arm hairs over and over. It's not pleasant, but there are many things more painful than this.

"While we're on the subject of my son," Ellen says. "You apologized at the memorial service for not being able to save Charlie, but please, don't do that ever again. Not to me, or anyone. My son died out of his time, but that doesn't mean you have to carry a lifetime of guilt." She pats my shoulder with a latex-gloved hand. "Release it. Let it go."

I can't say the guilt just goes away, but I do feel as if I've been given permission to stop playing the endless *what if . . .* game in my head.

"And while I have you trapped here under the needle—" Charlie's mom doesn't wait for me to say thank you. "The other thing you need to know is how much your mother loves you. Almost every time we spoke on the phone, she was on her way to the one store in town that sells the most

comfortable socks or the warmest undershirts or your favorite candy."

The tattoo machine goes silent as she loads the needles with more ink.

"I can't tell you that losing my son didn't unravel me," she says. "But the last thing he told me before he was killed was that he loved me. It brings me comfort to remember that. Travis, there is no one in this world your mother loves more than you. Not your dad. Not your brother. You. If anything were to happen, she would be—"

"I know."

"Be gentle with her." Again, she pats my shoulder. "And thus endeth the lecture."

She works in silence for a while, until Harper and Jenny come downstairs. Harper stands behind me for a moment or two, watching, then sits on a second stool, pulling it up in front of me until her knees are touching mine. "I like it."

"Good."

"Harper, I'd be delighted if you'd let me give you a tattoo," Charlie's mom says. "Whatever you want."

"I appreciate the offer," she says. "But one is enough for me."

Wait. What? Harper has a tattoo?

"You have a tattoo?" I ask.

"Yep."

I've seen her in a pair of shorts and a bikini top, so there aren't many places she could have hidden ink—which kind

of turns me on. As much, you know, as I can be when I'm being repeatedly jabbed with needles. "Why haven't I seen it?"

Harper laughs. "Because I haven't shown it to you yet."

"Can I see it later?"

"I'm not going to talk about this right now." Her face goes pink, so her tattoo must be in a really good spot. "Forget about it."

Behind me, Charlie's mom chuckles as she draws the ink lines on my back. Just forget about it? Not when my imagination is taking me to many interesting body parts. "Is it a turtle?" I ask.

"Good guess," Harper says. "But no."

"Chinese symbol?"

She scrunches her nose. "Ew."

"Does it have something to do with Charley Harper?"

"Possibly," she says, but she fights a smile that tells me it does.

"Nice choice," Ellen tells her over my shoulder. "I love tattoos that have some originality behind them. Don't get me wrong, my bread and butter comes from tramp stamps and tribal bands, but there is nothing better than doing a custom piece or a design that took some reflection."

"What is it?" I ask Harper. I googled Charley Harper once. His style was a little cartoonish and he specialized in nature. Especially birds.

"You'll find out when you find out."

When Ellen finishes, she swabs the blood and ink off my skin, then hands me a mirror so I can see the reflection. As far as tattoos go, it's a good one. "Thank you," I say. "For everything."

She tapes a bandage over it and after I pull my shirt back on, she gives me a hug. "Thank *you* for offering up your skin just to humor me," she says. "You might find a tattoo a much easier way than guilt to carry Charlie with you."

Chapter 16

It's still early when we return to the hotel. There's a message on my phone from Kevlar, inviting us to a motel out at the beach where most of the Marines from Kilo are staying. There's talk of kiteboarding and darts at some English pub. It's a guaranteed good time, and I'm ready for that.

"We can go, if you want," Harper says.

Except now—I don't know. I guess I'd rather spend time with her than hang out with a group of guys I'll see again in a couple of weeks. I know what kind of shit I'll get from Kevlar about this, but I don't care. I reach for her waist, drawing her in until her hips rest against mine. "I want to see your tattoo."

Her hand curls around the back of my neck and pulls my face down. She feathers kisses on my forehead, my cheeks, along my jawline, the spot just below my ear—her lips so fleeting my brain can barely register them before they've moved on. Shivers race up and down my spine like electricity. I could power the city. The state. The whole fucking world.

Harper sighs and touches her forehead to mine. "Travis?"

"Yeah?"

"I, um . . ." Her voice is a whisper. "I don't know if I can do this."

"Okay." I want her so much right now it hurts, but I don't want to be an asshole. So I swallow my frustration and kiss her forehead. "It's okay."

"I guess I'm a little . . . scared."

"Of what?"

"Everything," she says. "That it will be awkward and weird. Or I'll do it wrong. But mostly—well, mostly that I can't compare to Paige. She's beautiful and . . ." Harper glances down at her chest. "She has big boobs and—"

"There is no comparison," I interrupt. "*Everything* about you is better."

"You didn't think so in middle school."

"I was fourteen," I say. "I was thinking with the wrong head back then. As opposed to, you know, now. When I only think with the wrong head sometimes."

She laughs. A good sign.

"And, okay, to be completely honest?" I say. "I'm kinda nervous myself."

Her eyes go wide. "Really?"

Sex with Harper is going to be complicated. She's a happily-ever-after girl and I can't make that kind of promise when I'm only nineteen and owe the Marine Corps three more years of active duty. Anything could happen. She could dump me for some smart guy in her biology class at college and *that* Dear John letter wouldn't be nearly so easy to shake off. Or I could step on an IED on my next deployment and she—see, I'm thinking way too much about this.

But here's the thing: the strings are already attached.

"Yeah, well, it's my first time with *you* and I want to get it right." It sounds like a line. Like I'm trying to get in her pants. Which I am, but not the way it seems. Harper's skepticism registers in the hitch of her brows and it makes me laugh. "Okay, that sounded lame, but"—I drop my voice low because I have to admit something that kind of scares me—"I don't want to mess this up."

She gives me that tiny bit-lip smile that always knocks me out, and I know I've said the right thing.

"But"—I shoot her a grin—"if you want to wait, I'll live. Of course, my balls will probably shrivel up and fall off, but don't feel bad about that or anything."

Harper gives me a little punch in the gut, then circles her arms around my neck. Her lower lip grazes mine and, just before she kisses me, she tells me to shut up.

* * *

The wooden floorboards of the porch creak in the quiet darkness as I carry Harper's bag to the front door. We stand there a moment in the dim yellow glow of the porch light, a couple of idiots grinning at each other because things are different now. For one thing, I don't have the specter of my hookup with Paige lurking over my shoulder. For another, the memorial service is behind me.

Also, I've seen Harper's tattoo.

But it's not only that. On the drive home we played Slug Bug, punching each other every time we saw a VW Beetle. Tried Guinness-flavored ice cream. And stopped to eat at this pirate adventure dinner theater place in Orlando, where we watched a Broadway-style swashbuckler show about a princess taken hostage by pirates. It was goofy to a degree that should have been embarrassing, but it wasn't. It was fun.

Normal.

I don't know if my life will ever be completely normal again, but something like normal is a good start.

"Thanks for coming with me," I say. "And, you know, just being there."

"What can I say?" She gives me a smart-ass little grin as she shrugs. "I kinda like you."

"Kinda?" I wrap my arms around her, my lips next to her ear. "I call shenanigans."

She turns her face toward me so I can kiss her, and we're making out when the door opens. Her dad is on the other side of the screen. He runs his hand through his bed-head hair and squints sleepily at the light. "You're home."

"Yes, sir."

"Does this public display of affection with my daughter on my front porch mean I'm stuck with you now?" he asks, opening the screen door for Harper.

I'm not sure if I should laugh, so I hold back. "I'm afraid so."

He chuckles and shakes my hand. "Thanks for bringing her home in one piece. Now go home and don't come back until the sun has been up for at least several hours."

When I get to my own house, my mom is curled up in the corner of the family room couch, watching her favorite old black-and-white movie.

I sit down beside her and she offers me her bowl of popcorn. I take a handful and clear my throat. "I, um—think I forgot to thank you for everything you sent me while I was in Afghanistan."

"I turned it into a game, trying to find the best and most useful things," she says. "I had so much fun."

I shovel in the popcorn and talk with my mouth full. "Next time, send more porn."

"Travis!"

"I'm kidding," I say. "But you know what would have been awesome? Tuna. I'd have killed for a tuna fish sandwich."

"Why didn't you tell me?"

"I don't know," I say. "I guess I didn't want to come off as ungrateful, especially since I sucked at keeping in touch."

Her face goes serious. "I'm not going to pretend my feelings weren't hurt, but I'd have sent you anything you wanted. You're my son, Travis, and I love you."

"I love you, too."

We sit in silence for a few moments while the princess in the movie gets a haircut so no one in Rome will recognize her.

"I was a jerk about Dad and I'm sorry," I say. "It's not really my business. And I've got your back whatever you decide."

"I filed the papers."

"I can't say that makes me sad," I say. "But are you going to be okay?"

"Now?" She smiles at me. "Absolutely."

Chapter 17

Charlie,

    I know you can't read this, but I've been seeing a therapist and she thought I should write about you. Instead, I thought it might be easier to write to you. Maybe we're both wrong, and either way I feel kind of stupid writing to a dead person, but I figured I'd give it a try.

    I've been diagnosed with post-traumatic stress disorder, but just talking to a therapist doesn't make it magically disappear. I mean, it's good to unload some of the stuff I've been carrying around in my head, but I still have nightmares. I still wake up in the middle of the night, sweaty and scared, and have to remind myself it's not real. The thing is, she tells me that the nightmares may never go away. That it could take years to stop reacting to loud noises or scanning the ground for IEDs. And even though I haven't seen you in a while, I'll probably never stop mistaking strangers in crowds for you. It sucks, but I'm learning to deal.

A lot of things have changed since you've been gone. My parents split and my dad moved back to Green Bay. That's what my mom tells me, anyway. I don't talk to him, he doesn't talk to me, and that seems to work for both of us. Mom sold the house and got a smaller place. She spends most of her time collecting supplies for Afghan kids, but she's been up to see your mom and Jenny a couple of times.

Speaking of your mom, I went to see her like I promised. You were right about her. She's kind of weird, but in a good way. You'd have laughed your ass off when Kevlar found out she's a lesbian. By the way, Kevlar finally got laid, but you really don't want to know those details.

Remember how I joked about doing the recon course? Turns out, Kevlar went instead and he's with First Recon out of Pendleton now. Ever since Afghanistan he's been living from adrenaline rush to adrenaline rush, so I hope this works for him. The last time we talked, which has been a while, he claimed to have a seriously hot girlfriend but won't show me any pictures, so I call shenanigans. She's probably a whale.

Anyway, I ended up being sent to bomb dog school. At first I was against it because it means going out on more patrols when we go back to Afghanistan, but dude . . . this is probably the coolest thing I've ever done. My dog is a black Lab named Bodhi, which your mom says is a Sanskrit word that means "awakening" and claims it's a sign that he is the right dog for me. I'm not sure that's true, but I like him a lot. Bodhi is finishing up some training while I'm on leave, so I won't see him again until the airport. I'm not saying I want to go back to that shithole of a country, but I'm looking forward to working with my dog again.

Right now, I'm in Maine visiting my new girlfriend, Harper. I'm not sure how this whole long-distance thing is going to work, but she says she'll be here when I get back. I have to believe, though, because that's the kind of girl she is. You'd really like her and I know she'd like you, too.

Maybe you know all this stuff already. Maybe you're hanging with the Buddha, watching us try to figure out how life is supposed to work without you. But if you don't know, it's not easy. Sometimes it feels like I've left the water running or

forgot to lock the door, and then I remember
and it sucks all over again. Maybe someday we'll see
each other again, Charlie. For real, I mean. Until
then, save me a seat, okay?

~Solo

ACKNOWLEDGMENTS

Thanks to . . .

The 3rd Battalion 6th Marines, whose experiences in Afghanistan shaped this book. And to Clint Van Winkle, whose book *Soft Spots: A Marine's Memoir of Combat and Post-Traumatic Stress Disorder* was enormously inspiring.

Maximilian and Didie Uriarte for letting me ask the questions and the members of Terminal Lance (especially MoMo) for answering.

SSgt. Zachary Strelke, LCpl. Ceejay Maxwell, Cpl. Ben Harris, LCpl. Ben Lyons, Sgt. Alex Piasecki, Cpl. Cliff "Ski" Kralewski, Sgt. Jeremy Goldman, LCpl. Jared Perumal, Tony Rash, and US Army Master Sgt. Jarrod Griffith for going above and beyond. And all the thanks in the world is not enough for LCpl. David Backhaus.

Bloggers Danielle Benedetti, Carla Black, Chelsea Swiggett,

Adele Walsh, and Gail Yates for being my personal cheerleading squad. You are all totally awesome.

Mahnoor Yahwar for helping me navigate Islamic customs, letting me borrow one of your kissing stories, and being a wonderful friend. (You have dibs.)

Josh Berk, Tara Kelly, Miranda Kenneally, Amy Spalding, Cheryl Macari, and the crew of Barnes & Noble 2711 in Fort Myers, Florida, for support, advice, critiques, and—the best part—the friendships.

Suzanne Young for everything. I don't know what I'd do without you.

My agent, Kate Schafer Testerman, who believed in me—and Travis. I wouldn't have wanted to make this journey with anyone else.

Michelle Nagler at Bloomsbury for taking a chance on an uncommon protagonist, and Victoria Wells Arms for pushing when I didn't always want to be pushed. It was always in the right direction and ultimately led to a better book, and I'm so grateful for that.

My mom, Mary Singler, who cries when she reads this book and tells me she's proud. Thank you for helping me become someone of whom you could be proud.

Jack and Marilyn Doller for their love and support, and to Sharon Doller, who has made this journey in my heart.

Scott and Caroline, who are the best people I know. I hope one day you find something that fulfills you the same way writing does for me, no matter what it is.

And finally, Phil. Because I love you best of all.